# The Last Chance

# The Last Chance

*James Gauthier*
*and*
*Ed Martin*

iUniverse, Inc.
New York  Lincoln  Shanghai

# The Last Chance

iUniverse, Inc.

For information address:
iUniverse, Inc.
2021 Pine Lake Road, Suite 100
Lincoln, NE 68512
www.iuniverse.com

Illustrations: Frank Bolle and Bob Wiacek

ISBN: 0-595-27913-9

Dedicated to:

Linus, Percy, Brittney, Charles, Doora and Lefty

# Contents

# Acknowledgements

We would like to thank the following people for their support, encouragement, suggestions and kind words.

Joanne Gauthier, Ray Szwec, Kristen Ware, Sal Trapani, Mark Giannini, Lynn Britt, Will Butler, Matt Barry, Kristen Sueoka, Aaron Hayes, Dave Chandler, RJ Katz, Lanae Blethen, Logan Rummel, Kenny Megan, Joan Levy Hepburn, Nathan Blue, Nico Raineau, Andrew Karpov, Remy Zaken, Jason Vitagliano, Greg Vitagliano, Erik Vitagliano.

Bishop

Mandy

Gary

Justin

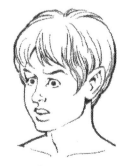

Aquarian

Christie Rae Mann

Onyx

Alabaster

Random

Andrew Chance

Print

Reprint

# Prologue

## Twenty Years Ago

A towering medieval castle scraped the night sky, standing strong as it had for centuries against a raging storm. There was no rain, only gale-force winds and frequent blasts of neon colored lightning accompanied by loud crackling noises rather than the thunder Earth people associate with similar violent weather. The lightning glared off the castle's exterior, a highly polished white marble that vividly reflected the rainbow of lightning colors.

Only the tower room windows were illuminated. In one of those windows, a silhouetted figure watched the glorious maelstrom. He was Alabaster, the king of this world. His lean build and thick head of straight, blond hair suggested that he was even younger than his 25 years. The look on his face, though, revealed that he carried the accumulated concerns of a much older man. Around him, several enormous windows afforded sweeping views in every direction. Outside those windows, the storm built in intensity, as if to foreshadow the events that were to come. Between the windows were portraits of the many leaders who had preceded Alabaster's rule.

Alabaster always thought his father's funeral would be the worst experience of his life. He was about to be proven wrong. The boom of a door slamming open ended his contemplation. Without turning around, he spoke, his voice barely containing his anger.

"What kept you, Onyx?"

Behind Alabaster, a much larger and more imposing figure slowly entered the room. The lines on his face made clear that he was a few years older than Alabaster. He, too, had a full head of hair, but it was black and thick, with white stripes above each temple. He spoke with an arrogance that rivaled his appearance.

"I owe you no explanation."

"We missed you at father's funeral."

There was an uncomfortable stillness in the air as Alabaster waited for his brother to reply. When it became clear that Onyx would remain silent, Alabaster continued. "We briefly delayed the services, on the assumption that you had been unavoidably detained."

"Then you are even bigger fools than I know you to be."

Alabaster turned to face a portrait on the wall. It was a painting of a beautiful young woman with long dark hair. She had a regal look about her.

"I'm glad mother isn't here to witness your thoughtlessness."

"You speak as if she's out of town on a holiday. Mother is long dead, Alabaster. I only wish father had joined her sooner."

For the first time, Alabaster's face betrayed the anger that he had been feeling. "You are rancid to the core, brother."

Onyx enjoyed taunting Alabaster. "With both of them out of the way, it is time for me to assume control of our kingdom."

"Father chose me."

"Father was old and senile," Onyx hissed. "His word will never hold."

"You lie. As ever."

"A competent man would never have selected you. You are not a leader! You are small and weak!"

"What you perceive as weakness, others would call compassion," Alabaster calmly replied.

"Compassion? Hah! Your words carry no power."

"Leave me, Onyx. I have work to do."

"I am the oldest male child and it is my birthright to lead the king-dom. If you will not give it to me voluntarily, then I shall have to take it by force." Onyx studied the ring on his right hand. It was solid gold with a shiny black stone in the center. Onyx twisted the ring and thrust his hand forward. A cobra suddenly appeared on a large wooden table next to Alabaster.

"Holograms?" Alabaster was not impressed.

Onyx smiled. "This is much more than a mere hologram, brother."

The cobra darted at Alabaster, its fangs tearing his left sleeve. Alabaster responded by twisting his own ring, which was gold with a white stone. A mongoose appeared on the table and immediately attacked the cobra.

"Your little toys can't help you, Onyx. I will always remain one step ahead of you."

Onyx stepped forward and shoved Alabaster, knocking him to the floor. He reached down and grabbed Alabaster by the collar, but Alabaster tore himself free and shoved Onyx into the table. The cobra and the mongoose evaporated. Onyx rolled to one side, reached into a pocket and produced a small black object, which quickly expanded into a black sword. He sprang to his feet. Alabas-ter also rose. The two brothers stared at each other.

"What are you waiting for, Alabaster? Arm yourself!"

Alabaster did nothing. With sudden, blinding speed, Onyx's sword slashed the air, grazing Alabaster's cheek. A thin line of blood appeared on his face. Alabaster did not move.

"I have no desire to harm you," Alabaster said.

"Then you are going to die!"

Onyx swung his sword. Alabaster dove to one side, avoiding con-tact. Onyx attacked again. It was another near miss, but enough to send Alabaster into action. He ran to his desk, pulled open a drawer and grabbed a small object similar to the one Onyx produced from his pocket. Within seconds, it too became a large sword—a shining white weapon.

"I knew you weren't a complete coward," Onyx sneered.

As thunder and neon lightning continued to crash outside the windows, the two men clashed, their mighty swords releasing showers of neon sparks on contact. Onyx finally succeeded in striking Alabaster's sword with such force that he lost his grip. The white sword scuttled across the floor as Alabaster fell. Onyx was on him in an instant, his black sword poised at Alabaster's throat.

Onyx was triumphant. "At last, I will finally have what is mine!"

Suddenly a gunshot rang out. "Who dares?" Onyx roared. He whirled around and saw Alabaster's trusted aide Castleton, a tall lanky man with curly white hair, standing in the doorway. He was holding the gun that had been fired.

With Onyx momentarily distracted, Alabaster rolled to the side, grabbed his sword and swung it at Onyx, striking his forearm. Onyx screamed and dropped his weapon. Seconds later, several guards rushed into the room and descended on the wounded Onyx.

Castleton dashed to Alabaster's side. "Are you okay, your majesty?

"I am now. Thank you, Castleton."

"I thought a gunshot might bring the guards running," Castleton said with a smile. "To say nothing of distracting your brother."

Onyx was enraged. "Now what are you going to do, Alabaster? Kill me? Or have me killed?"

"You are my brother. I cannot do either."

"Again your weakness overcomes you. Or would you call it your compassion?"

"Rather than kill you, I will banish you from the kingdom," Alabaster said. "The guards will be ordered to imprison you for life if you are found anywhere near my empire proper. Go, brother, and bother no one. You will not find me so forgiving in the future."

Onyx pulled himself free of the guards. He grabbed his wounded arm.

"This isn't over, Alabaster. One day, I will take what belongs to me!"

"You and what army?"

"You will see, brother. You will see." Onyx stormed out of the room. The guards followed close behind.

"Was it wise to let him go, your majesty?" Castleton asked.

"I can only do what I believe to be right."

"I fear we haven't seen the last of Onyx."

"I'm afraid you may be right, Castleton. I have a feeling that this will not end until one of us is dead."

# Chapter 1

## Don't Look Now

Twenty years later, on the planet Earth, young Bishop Chance silently watched as the sequence of events between Alabaster and Onyx unfolded once again. These visions had recently started and had been building in intensity. They always involved the same two men and they were always fighting. He had told nobody about the visions because he feared that people would think he was crazy. And he was afraid they might be right.

This latest vision ended with the sudden scream of a whistle. Bishop suddenly found himself standing at the edge of a large indoor pool wearing a bathing suit. He saw other boys in the pool swimming away from him. He was at a swim meet. He had been daydreaming once again. Daydreaming about these bizarre visions. He heard the whistle screech a second time, followed by the voice of his coach, who was yelling at him.

Bishop dove in, attempting to catch up with the other swimmers. But his dive was very sloppy and his stroke was compromised by his lack of focus.

Bishop remained in last place throughout the two-lap race. His coach stood at the side of the pool, clearly upset by Bishop's bad performance. In the stands, amid dozens of cheering students, sat Mandy Conway, a pretty brunette with sparkling blue eyes who could not stop watching Bishop. She looked worried.

"Oh, Bishop. Not again," Mandy sighed.

Bishop came in dead last. The swimmers climbed out of the water. Bishop remained in the pool and watched as the winner, Justin Wellington III, received congratulations from the coach. Mandy made her way toward the swimmers as the audience began to disperse.

The coach approached Bishop. "What the devil is your problem, Chance?"

"I'm sorry, coach. It won't happen again."

"You said that last week and the week before. Screw up again and you're off the team."

The coach stormed off. Now it was Justin's turn to belittle Bishop.

"Beat you again, Chance."

"Yeah. You're still the man, Justin."

"Why don't you give it up? You're holding back the whole team."

Justin went to speak with the coach as Bishop climbed out of the pool. He stood up and found himself face to face with Mandy.

Bishop's greeting was half-hearted. "Hi, Mandy. Here to see your boyfriend win again?"

"Justin is not my boyfriend. We're just friends."

"That's not the way he sees it."

Justin suddenly stepped between them. "I feel like celebrating. Let's hit the coffee house. My treat."

"Do they serve birthday cake?" Mandy asked.

"Huh?" came Justin's thoughtful response.

"It's Bishop's birthday."

"Happy birthday, I guess," Justin said, without enthusiasm.

"Don't worry, Justin," Bishop replied. "You two go ahead. I won't spoil your celebration. I have to get home, anyway. Gary's coming over."

"Yeesh! What a way to spend your birthday. With that load of lard!"

Mandy ignored Justin. "Is it okay if I come, too?"

Justin was stunned. "What? You'd rather go with that loser than with me?"

Now Bishop ignored Justin. "Uh, yeah, Mandy. Sure. That would be cool."

"Great! I'll meet you outside after you've changed."

A fuming Justin followed Bishop into the boys' locker room. As Bishop approached his locker, Justin walked up behind him.

"Hey, Chance. Don't even think about going after Mandy. I'm going with her to your stupid party."

Bishop didn't turn around. Being further ignored angered Justin.

"I'm going out with her, Chance! And it's gonna stay that way! Got it?"

There was still no response from Bishop. Justin flared. He grabbed Bishop by the shoulder and forcibly turned him around. They were nose to nose.

"I mean it!" Justin snarled.

Suddenly, the fluorescent lights above them crackled and exploded. Both boys jumped.

"What the heck was that?" Justin yelped. He turned to avoid the mess, only to step on a piece of broken glass. "Ow! Ouch! Ouch! I'm gonna get you for this, Chance! I hope your birthday sucks! I hope your whole life sucks! Ouch! Ow!"

Bishop couldn't help but smile as Justin hopped away, favoring his injured foot.

After he had changed, Bishop walked outside and found Mandy with the slightly injured Justin moping at her side.

Mandy smiled. "Let's go."

As they walked down the street, they noticed strange things occurring. Car alarms went off as they passed by and the overhead streetlights flickered. At each intersection traffic lights blinked red, yellow and green and walk signals flashed on and off. There were numerous accidents as cars shot through traffic lights that were green on all four sides.

Mandy grew uneasy. "What's going on around here?" she asked.

"Wellington Light & Power must be having a melt down," Bishop said.

Justin scowled. He knew that Bishop's comment was meant to irritate him since it was widely known in town that Wellington Light and Power was one of the many companies his family owned.

Two cars screeched to a halt nearby, narrowly avoiding a collision. Mandy jumped. Bishop attempted to calm her, but Justin wedged himself between them. Justin faced Bishop.

"I hope you're not expecting any birthday presents, Chance."

"Presents!" Mandy gasped. "I totally forgot about presents!"

"Mandy, you don't need to get me anything."

"Yes I do, Bishop. We both do. It's your birthday!"

Justin frowned. "Did I not just indicate that I was not getting Chance a present?"

"Come on, Justin. We've got to buy Bishop a present."

"What?"

"We'll meet you at your house, Bishop." Mandy grabbed the protesting Justin and pulled him away. As Bishop watched them leave a streetlight above him crackled and exploded.

Left alone, Bishop continued walking until he reached his home. It was an old colonial house that had been in his mother's family for four generations. It had fallen into disrepair over the past thirteen years since the death of his parents. His grandfather was too old to make any improvements, and they couldn't afford to hire anyone to do them.

As always, the back door was unlocked. Bishop entered the kitchen. His grandfather was sitting at the table reading the newspaper, his silver hair illuminated by the afternoon sun.

"Hi, Grandpa," Bishop said. He put his gym bag on the counter and bounded to the fridge.

"Bag off the counter," came the curt reply.

Bishop complied.

"If you're looking for a soda, we're out," Andrew Chance grumbled. "I asked you to pick some up at the store."

"Sorry. I forgot. I'll get it later."

Andrew put down his newspaper. "You're forgetting everything lately. How did you do in your swim meet?"

"Uh, okay."

"I've heard that before. Don't tell me you came in last again?"

"Yeah. I did." Bishop knew what was coming. He looked down at the floor as the usual lecture began.

"Bishop, this is not a game. This is your life. Do you want to spend it forgetting things and coming in last all the time?"

"No."

"Then you had better straighten up and get your head out of the clouds. I know I sound a little harsh, but it's for your own good. You don't want to turn out like your father."

"Don't start on dad again!" Bishop snapped, surprised at the sudden anger in his voice.

"Bishop, I have—rather, I had—a great deal of respect for your father. But he was a lot like you. And look what happened to him. Killing himself and your mother in a car crash."

Andrew stood and walked to the back door.

"I'm going to the senior center. We'll have your birthday dinner when I get back. By the way, your fat friend is waiting for you in the living room. He's always over here. Doesn't he have a home of his own?"

Andrew exited as Bishop entered the living room. Gary O'Leary was seated on the burnt orange couch, the centerpiece of the room that had the look of the mid-Seventies: A disturbing riot of faded yellow, green, orange and brown tones.

Gary's stomach pressed against the white wooden coffee table as he stared intently at an open lap top computer. A lollipop dangled from his mouth.

Bishop only had one true friend, and that was Gary, whose girth sometimes came in handy. Since Bishop had always been slight of build, bigger kids had picked him until Gary stepped into his life. Although Gary was chubby, he was also somewhat muscular.

"Hey, Bish. Happy B-Day. How'd the meet go?"

"I screwed up. Again."

"What's up with that, dude?"

"I was thinking about my father."

"Again?"

"Yeah, it's weird. Lately I can't stop thinking about him. All the time. It's almost like he's trying to talk to me, or something."

"That's bizarre."

"It's even weirder than that," Bishop continued. "I haven't told you before, but I've been having visions of my father. He's always fighting someone in an old castle. I can't understand it."

"That's nothing," Gary replied. "I used to make up all sorts of stories about my family when I was a kid."

"Yeah, but I'm not a kid. I'm fourteen. I wish I knew what was going on."

"Why don't you ask the crabby old geezer?"

Bishop laughed. "Hey, I can call my grandfather a crabby old geezer. You can't."

"Sorry. Just calling it like I see it."

"My grandfather doesn't like to talk about my folks. Ever. Except to remind me that he blames my father for the death of my mother."

The two were quiet for a moment. Bishop picked up a stack of envelopes from a nearby table, and then sat next to Gary, who was still busy typing. Bishop began to open one envelope.

"Did Mandy send you a birthday card?"

"Yep. It says, Happy 14th, Stud-Boy."

Gary reached for the card. "Yeah. Right. Lemme see."

Bishop held it away. "No way. It's private!"

"Well, don't let Justin see it. He'll go ballistic."

"I don't care what Justin does."

Gary was suddenly distracted by something on the computer screen.

"What's wrong?" Bishop asked.

"I don't believe it! The stupid computer just crashed! I was just about to hack into the school's system! That was going to be my birthday present to you. Straight A's." Gary frowned as he studied the computer. Without thinking he reached into his pocket, pulled out another lollipop and inserted it into his mouth.

"Thanks but no thanks," Bishop said. "Don't be giving me any phony A's."

"Come on, man. You said your grades took a dive this semester. Wouldn't you like to bring home something better than a C average?"

"I'm not gonna cheat."

"Well, then, I could give Justin straight D's."

Bishop was suddenly enthusiastic. "Yeah? Cool."

Gary was still punching at the keys. He looked increasingly perturbed. "It isn't going to happen," he groaned. "This piece of junk is dead!"

"It can't be dead. It's only a few months old. Maybe it just froze."

Bishop took the computer in his hands and shook it. "C'mon, computer. Work!" Suddenly, the laptop put forth a series of loud beeps.

Gary was wide-eyed. "Hey! You did it!" As the laptop continued beeping, a buzzing noise from across the room further surprised the boys.

"What is that?" Gary asked.

"I don't know." Bishop handed the laptop to Gary. "Here. Ruin Justin's life." As Bishop stood, the laptop emitted a beep. There was also another loud beep from across the room. Bishop looked toward the source of the noise: An old computer on a desk in the corner. "Grandpa must have left his computer on," Bishop said.

"Whoa! Check it out!" Gary beamed, pointing to the laptop. Bishop leaned forward. The words 'Wellington High School: Student Grade Listings' had appeared on the screen.

"You got in! Cool!"

Another beep from the old computer again distracted Bishop. He walked toward it.

"Looks like your pal Justin got a B+in history," Gary smiled, his eyes fixed on the laptop.

"So give him a D! That'll fix his butt."

Bishop was now at the old computer. He was surprised to see the screen illuminated, filled with mysterious gibberish. He looked at the on/off button. It was in the off position. Bishop was puzzled. "The switch must be broken," he said.

Gary was also perplexed. "Something weird is going on here, Bish. Justin's history grade just changed to a D. But I didn't type anything."

"Maybe you read it wrong the first time. Maybe he really is a dope."

Bishop studied the laptop. "So if Justin already has a D, give him an F!"

Gary looked at the laptop screen and saw an instant F next to Justin's name.

"I swear there was a D there. First a B, then a D, now…"

Bishop was suddenly paranoid. "You know, we shouldn't be in those files. Maybe someone is tracking us, or something. Turn the computer off."

Before Gary could make a move, the laptop shut itself off. In that same instant, across the room the old computer emitted another series of loud beeps and its monitor went black.

"That old dinosaur over there is really acting up," Bishop said. "Guess Grandpa's been getting rough with it. He hates to lose at solitaire."

"Maybe grumpy gramps needs a new computer," Gary replied. "That wreck's at least 20 years old."

"It belonged to my parents. Just like everything in this house. Grandpa won't get rid of any of it. Not one thing."

Gary looked around the room at the tacky Seventies décor. "That's obvious."

The doorbell rang. Bishop dashed to the door. Mandy and Justin had arrived. Mandy handed Bishop a small wrapped package.

"Happy birthday, Bishop."

Justin also produced a package. It was a bakery box.

Bishop was sarcastic. "Gee, buddy, I didn't know you cared."

"This was Mandy's idea. A cake is not a gift. Are we clear?"

Mandy walked over to Gary. "What are you guys doing?"

"Uh, just some computer game stuff." Gary eyed the bakery box Justin was holding and tried to think of a way of getting the first piece of cake.

Justin knew this look. "Eyes off the cake, Jumbo," he sneered. "This is for Chance."

"Bite me, Wellington."

Mandy stepped between Justin and Gary. "Come on, guys. Cool it."

Justin turned to Bishop. "Mandy made me send you an email birthday greeting on my palm pilot. Did you get it?"

"Let me check." Bishop sat by the laptop and pushed the on button. "I hope you work this time, computer," he mumbled. As the laptop clicked on, the old computer across the room beeped to life again, too. Everyone looked at it. "I wish I knew what was going on with that thing," Bishop sighed.

The old computer beeped again. Bishop walked over to it. "What is this? Voice command response? Maybe Grandpa has been updating you on the side. Let's see what you have on your directory."

Bishop began typing, but after he hit a couple of keys the screen filled with an unknown language. "More gibberish? How am I supposed to find out what's inside of you if I can't understand you?"

"Now switching to audio mode," came a voice from the computer's speakers.

Bishop stepped back. "Whoa! Since when can you talk?"

"Since you expressed the need for further communication," the computer replied.

Bishop was now inexplicably engaged in a conversation with this machine. "Wait a minute! You can understand what I'm saying?"

"Your verbal input is acceptable."

"Are you utilizing some new program my grandfather installed?"

"Negative. Your father is the only person who has made modifications to my system."

Bishop's friends drew closer as the dialogue continued. "My grandfather said my father built you."

"Affirmative."

"Um, do you have any of his programs stored in your memory?"

"I have over 250,000 programs from Alabaster in my memory."

"Alabaster? Who's that?"

"Your father. His name was Alabaster. He changed it to Alan Chance when he came to this world and married your mother."

"What's going on here?" Mandy asked.

Bishop answered quietly. "I wish I knew."

"And so you shall," the computer replied. "Accessing file. Please wait for holographic video."

The monitor turned blue. Moments later, a three dimensional image formed behind a disbelieving Bishop. It was Alabaster, looking only slightly older than he had when he had banished Onyx from his kingdom those many years ago. His long blond hair was unkempt and he looked like he hadn't slept for a long time. The image began to speak.

"My son, the only way you could be hearing this is if I am not there in person."

"Dad?" Bishop's eyes teared up. He tried to touch the image, but his hand went right through it. Gary, Mandy and Justin could only stare.

"This is the story of my hopes and my failures. I should begin by telling you that I was not born on Earth. I came from what you might refer to as a parallel universe."

A smaller image of a shiny white marble medieval style castle appeared to Alabaster's right.

"What you are seeing to my right is my kingdom, which I ruled over when my father passed the throne to me. I tried to rule the people as he did, with kindness and compassion. The only challenge I faced was from my older brother, Onyx. He was angry because our father did not give him what he felt was his birthright."

Justin couldn't contain himself any longer. "Fess up, Chance. You downloaded this from the 'net, right? It's from one of those science-fiction geek Web sites, isn't it?"

It was Gary who responded. "It's a hologram, dork. You can't download a hologram."

The image of the castle changed to a man dressed in black.

"This is Onyx," Alabaster continued. "Your uncle."

Bishop was excited. "That's the guy I see my father fighting all the time in my visions," he whispered to Gary.

"Onyx refused to help me rule our people with civility," Alabaster continued. "He felt that the people were there for him to do with as he pleased. After our father died, I banished him from the kingdom. I am sorry to say that I underestimated Onyx. In the years that followed, he secretly built an army of outcasts. One day his army stormed the kingdom. A terrible battle ensued, and many lives were lost on both sides. We were able to defeat Onyx, but he was growing too powerful. I was working with my best scientists to devise a plan to stop him once and for all when, quite by accident, we created a portal into another world. This world, as we were to find out later, was Earth. Your world."

The image of Onyx changed to one of the Earth.

"Believing that I might learn new ways to defeat Onyx, I recruited several loyal aides from my court and decided to explore this new world, leaving others behind to keep Onyx at bay while we were away. Something quite remarkable happened when we arrived here. Each one of us acquired a different and unique power or ability that we did not have back home."

The image of the Earth changed into that of a beautiful young woman.

"Shortly after my arrival on Earth I met a woman whose beauty I cannot describe. We began spending a great deal of time together. We were wed after a brief courtship."

"Mom," Bishop said softly. He was crying now. Bishop was very young when his mother died. He had no memories of her, and yet, here she was.

The woman in the image was holding a baby. "One year later, you were born."

More tears rolled down Bishop's face as the image changed back to Alabaster.

"Unbeknownst to me, Onyx and his emissaries followed us through the portal. The strain was too much, and the portal imploded just after they arrived. My world is safe, as long as Onyx remains on Earth. The only way he has of getting back is through a new portal that only I can create. If you are watching this, my son, then I have passed on. It is your birthright to return to my world and become its rightful ruler. I have hidden a device that will let you open a portal. But Onyx must never find it. I shall lead you to it through a series of clues. Each clue will bring you closer to your goal. Don't worry. My people will be there to help you. But be very careful of Onyx and his emissaries. They also acquired powers as they came into this world, and they will use them against you to get what they want. They must not return to the Homeworld!"

Bishop and his friends remained transfixed as Alabaster continued. "As I record this message to you, you are still just an infant and have shown no signs of any special power. Perhaps you have taken after your mother and you will be a normal earthling. Or perhaps your power may take longer to emerge. If so, it will eventually present itself—later in childhood, or when you become an adult. Use it well, and use it for the good of others. Here is the first clue in your search for the device that will open the portal. For you to succeed in your plan, you must first see our man. Good-bye Bishop. Your mother and I love you very much. Don't look to the night sky to find your true home, my son. Look inward. Always remember, you are the last Chance."

Bishop wiped the tears from his eyes as the image faded away. "Good-bye, dad," he whispered.

Once again, Justin couldn't keep quiet. "I gotta hand it to you, Chance. You sure know how to put on a show."

"End of file," the computer said. "Do you wish to see another?"

"Computer, do you know anything about this mysterious man Bishop needs to meet?" Mandy asked. The computer didn't respond.

"You ask it, Bish," Gary said. "You're the one it likes."

Bishop composed himself. "Computer, are you programmed to take verbal commands only from me?"

"I was programmed to take verbal commands from Alabaster only. Your power must enable you to control electronic devices. That is what allows you to communicate with me and command me. It also gives you access to any program contained within my memory."

"How did my father know I'd be able to access his message? I mean, if you were programmed to accept verbal commands only from him? He didn't know I would have this power."

"I am programmed to communicate with Bishop Chance on the date of his eighteenth birthday, alerting him to Alabaster's message."

Bishop frowned. "So we're early."

"Kids grow up fast these days," Gary said as he produced a fresh lollipop from his pocket.

"Is there anything else you can tell me, computer?"

"Only that your father has placed a great deal of trust in you and that you will require all of your skills and all that he has left behind for you to complete your mission. The objects are in the possession of your father's most trusted aide. Find his aide, and you shall have what you seek."

"Who is this man?" Bishop asked. "Where can I find him?"

"All information regarding your father's operatives has been erased from my central information bank to protect them from Onyx."

"Can you tell us where we can find Onyx?"

"Onyx's whereabouts are unknown at this time."

The chatty computer fascinated Mandy. "He's cute. We should give him a name."

"You think I should give the computer a name?" Bishop asked.

"I already have a name," the computer replied, as if commanded by Bishop. "You may call me C.H.I.P."

"Why C.H.I.P?" Bishop asked.

"Complete Holographic Imagery Processor. C.H.I.P. for short."

The ring of an old rotary telephone in the Chance's kitchen suddenly distracted Bishop. He excused himself and left to answer it. Mandy could hear him talking in the other room. She turned to Gary, who was busily trying to type commands into C.H.I.P. with no success.

"Why are you bothering, Gary?" Mandy asked. "C.H.I.P. will only talk to Bishop."

"Hey. Anything Bish can do I can do, too. I just need a few minutes to figure this out. Bish always comes to me for help on his computer. This should be a breeze."

Mandy was miffed. "Why do you always try to outdo Bishop?"

Gary ignored her. "Why can't I do this?" he growled, pounding the keys in frustration.

"Maybe because Alabaster didn't want you to," Mandy replied.

"You don't believe all that sci-fi stuff, do you?" asked an incredulous Justin. "The father from another planet? Chance having freaky powers? This is all some kind of trick. Either Chance is pulling a fast one on us, or someone is pulling a fast one on him."

Bishop returned from the kitchen. "That was Miss Mann, my English teacher. She wanted to know if I could meet her at school and help her move some things to the drama department storage room. She sounded sort of desperate. I told her I'd do it. I said you guys would help, too."

"On a Saturday? No way!" Justin barked. He wasn't thrilled at the idea of going back to the school building. He had already been there earlier in the day for the swim meet.

"I'll go with you, Bish," Gary offered.

"So will I," Mandy said. "I like Miss Mann. And I think it's nice of you to help her, even on your birthday."

Justin felt threatened as always. He turned to Mandy. "If you're going, I'm going, too."

"Great, you can carry the cake!" Mandy smiled.

Justin picked up the cake and walked to the front door. "Lucky me. I get to go to school on Saturday afternoon! How could my day get any worse?" As Justin reached the door, he let out a yelp and grabbed his butt. "Oww!!"

"What's wrong?" Mandy asked.

"My pager just gave me a shock," Justin said, before yelping a second time. He pulled the device from his back pocket. "What's wrong with this thing?"

Justin and Mandy were both focused on Justin's pager as they left the house. Gary and Bishop lagged behind on the porch. Bishop was smiling.

"You did that, didn't you?" asked a disbelieving Gary. Bishop didn't answer. "This is all real, isn't it? For real. Really real." Bishop simply nodded, locked the door and followed Mandy and Justin. Gary watched his friend for a moment. "This is gonna be wild," he said to himself.

Bishop, Gary, Mandy and Justin strolled down the front walk, each filled with a sense of excitement and wonderment over the revelations of the day. They might have felt differently had they seen the pair of fiery red eyes watching them from Bishop's living room window.

# Chapter 2

## It's Always the Last Place You Look

As Bishop, Gary, Mandy and Justin were walking to school, Gary convinced the others that he needed to stop at his parents' store. So they made a slight detour to O'Leary's Confectionaries.

"I'll just be a minute," Gary said. "I need to grab something to eat."

"What else is new?" Justin asked.

Justin looked at the small store that was sandwiched between Wellington Dry Cleaners and Wellington Antiques; both owned and operated by his family. On the front of the store was a large window with the words O'Leary's Confectionaries painted in different colors.

Gary's parents, Mary and Barry O'Leary, were working behind the counter. Fresh baked goods were displayed in the counter case and on top. Jars of candy lined the shelves along the walls. Gary's ten-year-old brother Jerry was also working. Justin noted that all of the O'Leary's with the exception of Jerry were somewhat chubby.

Gary joined his brother as Mandy and Justin sat at the counter. Bishop went to the restroom to wash his hands.

Mrs. O'Leary bustled over to Mandy and Justin. "Hello, Mandy," she said. "Who's your friend?"

Gary answered for Mandy. "Oh, that's just Justin, ma." He pulled a jar of candy from one of the shelves. "I've told you about him."

"Nice to meet you, Justin." Mary turned to Gary. "Don't forget to take enough candy for your brother, dear."

Gary stopped in mid grab. "Mom, I can't take Jerry with me today. I've got important things to do."

His mother shook her head. "Well, you'll have to do your important things with him. Your father and I have to go out later and we need you to watch him for us."

"It's not fair," Gary grumbled, popping a jawbreaker into his mouth.

Mrs. O'Leary turned to Mandy. "You look so thin, dear. You must be starving. Jerry, will you please make Mandy a chocolate shake?"

"Comin' right up, ma," Jerry replied. As he set about the task at hand, his friend Jade and her brother Kenny entered the store. Jade was wearing a baseball shirt and carrying a bat. Even though Jade and Kenny were twins they did not look very much alike. Jade had long blonde hair, while Kenny's hair was brown. Also, Jade was several inches taller than Kenny, which made him appear to be younger. Jerry had had a crush on Jade since the third grade.

Jerry greeted them. "Hey guys, what are you doing here?"

"We decided to come in for some ice cream before my big game today," Jade said.

"Big game! Big deal!" Kenny snarled.

"It's not my fault that you're too small to make the team," Jade replied with a calculated smile.

Jerry looked at his mother. "Can I go to Jade's game today?"

"You were supposed to go with Gary," Mary replied.

"I don't want to hang out with him. I want to go with my friends."

"Sounds like a good idea to me," a relieved Gary piped in.

Mary shook her head. "I guess I'm outnumbered. Okay, Jerry, you can go with your friends." Mary then placed a plate of cookies and a bowl of candy on the counter in front of Mandy and Justin. "Here's something to nibble on until the shake is ready," she offered.

Mandy broke off a tiny piece of cookie and popped it into her mouth. Gary grabbed a handful of lollipops from another jar and shoved them into his pocket.

"Hey, Jerry, I want some ice cream," Kenny said. "I'll have vanilla cookie dough."

"Um, sorry, man, we're fresh out," Jerry replied.

Barry turned to his son. "What are you talking about, Jerry? We got a new shipment of vanilla cookie dough yesterday. How can we be sold out?"

Jerry was sheepish. "Well, maybe we didn't sell all of it. I might have eaten some."

"Some?" Barry asked.

"Okay, so maybe I ate all of it. But we still have lots of other flavors left."

"Maybe you should make that milkshake your mother asked you to make," Barry fumed.

Jerry scurried over to the milkshake machine and started it just as Bishop returned from the restroom. As Bishop approached, the blender surged and drenched Jerry in chocolate shake.

Mary was startled. "Jerry! Be careful!"

Jerry licked some of the shake from around his mouth. "Hmm. Not bad."

"I've got to call the power company about these surges," Barry grumbled. "They've been happening all day."

Mary changed the subject. "I haven't wished you a happy birthday, Bishop!" she smiled.

"Thanks, Mrs. O."

"I baked you a cake, but gremlins got into it." Mary frowned at a suddenly guilty looking Jerry and Gary. "I owe you one."

"Don't worry, Mrs. O," Mandy said. "Justin already brought a cake for Bishop."

Gary's pockets were now stuffed to capacity with candy. "I'm all set. Let's go."

Bishop and his friends got up from their seats and headed for the door.

"Give your grandfather our regards, Bishop," Mary said. "We haven't seen him around lately."

"Hey! What about Mandy's shake?" Jerry asked as Bishop and the others left the store.

"No thank you," Mandy called out as she stepped outside.

Seizing the moment, Jerry took a long swig of the shake. A room-shaking belch followed, drawing startled looks from everyone in the store.

"Oops," Jerry blushed. "Sorry."

Twenty minutes later, Bishop and his friends arrived at Wellington High School. They proceeded directly to a classroom on the first floor that was used for meetings of the drama club, where they were met by a statuesque woman. She was dressed in a white blouse; a short white skirt and white shoes and white boxes of various sizes surrounded her on all sides.

The woman smiled. "Hello, everyone. It's good of you all to come."

"Hi, Miss Mann," Bishop said.

"What's all this stuff?" Gary asked, eyeing the boxes.

"Just some things I haven't used in years. I'm donating them to the drama department. Since Bishop is a member of the drama club, I thought he could help me sort through it all."

"What's this?" Gary asked as he pulled a blue uniform from a box.

Miss Mann abruptly snatched the uniform from Gary. "That should have not been in there. A friend gave that to me many years ago. For safe-keeping."

Bishop was curious. "It looks like a costume."

Miss Mann was sly. "It's much more than that."

"What do you mean?"

Miss Mann looked at Gary, Mandy and Justin, and then turned back to Bishop. "I had hoped to talk to you alone about that, Bishop. It's a very important matter."

"Whatever it is, you can tell me in front of everyone. They're cool. Even Justin."

"He is?" Gary sniped. Gary always enjoyed sniping at Justin.

Miss Mann nodded. "Perhaps you are right. In fact, your chances may improve with their help."

"Chances?" Bishop asked. "Um, Miss Mann, what's going on here?"

Miss Mann spoke softly. "This uniform was given to me by someone very special. I grew up with him."

Mandy sensed the emotion in Miss Mann's voice. "Does he live in Wellington?"

"He did. He's...no longer with us. It's hard to believe that he's been dead almost thirteen years."

"Thirteen years?" Bishop sensed what was coming. "My father died thirteen years ago."

Miss Mann was now somewhat somber. "I know. That's who I was talking about."

"You mean you knew my father?"

Miss Mann nodded.

The sensitivity of the moment was lost on Justin. "Bishop's father used to wear that monkey suit? What was he? A circus clown?"

Miss Mann ignored him. "Your father and I went back a long time, Bishop."

"I was on my father's computer earlier. I heard some pretty incredible stuff."

"I know. You see, Bishop, long ago your father gave me a device that was designed to alert me that you had received his message. That wasn't supposed to happen until you were eighteen."

"Bishop's new power put things in high gear," Gary explained, sounding as if he were an expert on the subject.

"So your power has manifested itself?" Miss Mann asked. "What is it?"

Bishop turned and stared at Justin, who suddenly received another shock from the pager in his back pocket. Justin yelped, but he didn't drop the cake. Bishop gave him another jolt. There was more yelping. Mandy giggled. Gary laughed.

Justin was angry. "Are you doing that, Chance? Stop it!"

"What's going on?" Miss Mann asked. Bishop looked at the lights on the ceiling. They flickered as Bishop opened and closed his eyes.

"I see. You can control electronic devices," Miss Mann surmised.

"Yeah," Bishop replied. "It all started today."

"That would explain all the problems Wellington Light and Power has been having," Miss Mann mused.

"Hey, there is nothing wrong with my family's company," Justin snipped.

Bishop reiterated Alabaster's story. "The computer told me that my father came from another world and that he and all his friends have special powers. He also said that I need to return to his world and assume my birthright as its leader. But before I do that, I need to go on some type of quest and look for a device that will open a portal to his world. And he said I can't do that until I see his man."

Miss Mann was mesmerized. "See his man? Tell me exactly what he said, Bishop."

"He said in order for me to succeed in my plan, I must first 'see our man.'"

Miss Mann stood silent for a moment, a look of deep concentration settling on her face. Suddenly she smiled, chuckled and shook her head. "He wasn't saying that you should 'see' a 'man.' He was telling you to look for C.R. Mann! That's me! Christie Rae Mann. Also known as C.R. Mann. Your father enjoyed the occasional play on words."

"Are you saying that you are the aide we need to see?"

"Yes, Bishop. I'm afraid I asked you here today under false pretenses. I needed to verify that Alabaster's plan had been set in motion. I can't believe it is finally time to go into action. What a relief! I've only been pretending to be a school teacher all these years so I could keep track of your progress and report it to the others."

"How does that costume figure into this?" Gary asked. "Is Bishop going to be a superhero?"

"A superhero? Fat chance, Chance!" Justin laughed at his lame attempt at humor.

"The costume is woven from a fabric from our Homeworld. It will protect you, Bishop, against extreme heat and cold." Miss Mann reached into a box and pulled out a watch. "This is a remote link to your father's computer, or should I say C.H.I.P. You can access it from anywhere in the world as long as you have this."

Mandy looked around. "You didn't bring this stuff here to donate it to the drama department, did you? This is all for Bishop."

"Most of it, yes."

"But why bring all this stuff here?" Gary asked. "Wouldn't it have been easier to have Bishop go to your house?"

Miss Mann nodded. "Yes, it would have been easier for me, but not for Bishop. What I had to tell him was life-changing news. I wanted him to be in a familiar place when I told him. Bishop, I'm sure you feel more comfortable hearing the news here, rather than in strange surroundings."

"I guess." Bishop suddenly looked very serious. "You said that you were alerted about my father's holographic message by some kind of device."

Miss Mann smiled. "Yes, I told you I was keeping track of your progress. Just before your father died, he gave me a ring. It notified me when you activated your father's secret files on C.H.I.P." Miss Mann extended her hand to display a large ring that was bathed in a soft green glow.

Mandy was dazzled. "Wow. It's beautiful."

"So, what about this quest I'm supposed to go on?" Bishop asked. "Are you going, too?"

"No, Bishop. I am needed right here in Wellington. We can't be sure exactly how much Onyx knows about you. My colleagues and I will do what we can to slow them down, but you and your friends must do this without me." Miss Mann turned to Gary, Mandy and Justin. "If any of you don't want to help him, tell me now and I'll erase all memory of this from your minds."

"You can do that?" Gary asked.

Miss Mann was abrupt. "I can do many things."

Mandy stared at Gary and Justin. "We're standing by Bishop! Right, guys?"

"Uh, sure," Gary said, somewhat hesitantly.

Justin followed. "Yeah! Of course! A Wellington never runs from a challenge!"

Miss Mann handed Bishop a ring. "The stone in this ring will shine white when one of us is close at hand. But if the stone should turn black, that means Onyx or one of his emissaries is near. Onyx is evil personified. He disappeared shortly after he arrived here. We haven't been able to track down where he has been hiding all these years."

Miss Mann then produced another object. "Finally, you should take this dagger. It can cut through almost anything."

Bishop took the knife. "What do we do next?"

"I can't tell you, Bishop. You and your friends must figure that out for yourselves."

"Miss Mann, if you're from this other world, you must have a power, right?" Mandy asked.

Gary corrected Mandy, or so he thought. "Uh, she already said she could erase memories."

"That is one of my minor abilities," Miss Mann replied. "When the time comes, you will find out what my primary power is. Now go back to Bishop's house. I'll meet up with you there shortly. Your quest awaits. Please be careful. All of you." Miss Mann opened the door and left the room.

"This is all too weird," Justin said. "I think Miss Mann has lost her marbles."

"I don't," Bishop replied. "I can't explain why, but I really believe she's telling the truth. C'mon. Let's get back to my house. Maybe C.H.I.P. can help us."

As the four young adventurers once again walked through town they began to worry about the practical aspects of the challenges that were to come.

"How am I going to explain this to my parents?" Gary asked. "I can't just go up to them and say, 'Mom, Dad, I'll be back in a month or two. I've got to help Bishop claim his birthright as ruler of another planet.'"

"Don't worry, Gar," Bishop said. "We'll figure out something."

Mandy looked around. "Hey! The street lights aren't flickering anymore."

"I guess my power has settled in," Bishop surmised. The foursome had arrived at his house. Justin slowed as they approached the front porch.

"Having second thoughts, creepo?" Gary asked.

"I...I'm just not sure I want to waste...I mean...spend my time helping Chance," Justin replied. He was still carrying the bakery box with Bishop's cake inside.

"Wuss," Gary mumbled.

Justin shot back. "Go eat something, tubbo."

"All right, guys. Knock it off, okay?" Bishop said as he unlocked his front door and stepped inside. Before the others could enter, they heard Bishop cry out, "Hey! Who are you?"

Without hesitating, Gary and Mandy raced inside, leaving Justin alone. He heard sounds of a struggle coming from within the house.

"What's going on in there?" Justin said, meekly.

Suddenly two black-clad arms reached out the door, grabbed Justin and pulled him into the house. The cake dropped to the porch. "Hey! Get away from me! I'm a Wellington! Oww!!!" Justin cried from inside.

The door slammed, only to re-open moments later. The mysterious arms reached out, grabbed the cake and pulled it inside. "Chocolate. Yum, yum," said a gravely voice as the door slammed shut once again.

# Chapter 3
## Would I Lie?

A man wearing a black hooded robe escorted a blindfolded Bishop, Mandy, Gary and Justin into what appeared to be a cavernous underground room. Once their blindfolds were removed they found themselves surrounded by grotesque statues of men and women in various stages of torture. They appeared to be crying out in agony. Bishop could barely stand to look at them. He saw that Mandy had also gotten upset over the statues. He took her hand to comfort her.

At the front of the room were steps leading towards an ornate black throne. Fire billowed from pots positioned on each side. Torches lined the room. The place felt cold and damp, even with all the fire.

A deep threatening voice boomed, "Kneel! HE shall deal with you when HE arrives!"

The four were forced to their knees by skeletal hands reaching out from the surrounding darkness. Moments later a dark figure appeared from behind the throne. He was dressed in black from head to toe, with a flowing black cape behind him.

"My dear children, what are you doing on your knees?" the man asked. His face was hidden by shadows. "Please get up. Silhouette, how could you treat our guests in so contemptible a manner?"

Silhouette, the man in the black hooded robe who had brought them to this room, stepped out of the shadows and shuddered. "I am sorry, oh great Onyx."

"Onyx?" Gary exclaimed. "You're him! Bish! He's your uncle! Oh, gross."

"I must apologize for the way this place looks," Onyx said with an ugly chuckle. "It's so hard finding good help nowadays. I've been meaning to get some electricity down here for years, but something always seems to happen to the service people."

"I'll bet he eats them," Gary whispered to Bishop.

"I want to talk to you about why you are here as my guests," Onyx continued.

"Guests? I'd hate to see how you treat your prisoners!" Gary sneered.

"Yes, you would." Onyx flashed an evil smile.

"Where are we? What's going on?" Justin demanded. "I'll have you know my father is a very powerful man in this town! You'd better stop all this or you'll regret it!"

Onyx laughed. "I have no doubt that your father is a powerful man in Wellington. But let me warn you that I am the most powerful man in the world. For now, know only that I bear you no ill will. Perhaps you may have heard that I am an evil man. A corrupt man. Lies! All lies! Spread by my enemies, who are trying to deceive you!"

Bishop finally spoke. "Well, Uncle Onyx, the way you brought us here wasn't very hospitable."

"Yes, I know, nephew. But you see, there are individuals out there who would stop at nothing to discover my location. It was necessary for your safety, as well as my own, that none of you be aware of where you are at the moment. I know that you are about to embark on a quest. A very important quest. One that can lead me back to my home. I feel that we can both save a lot of time and energy if we combine forces and try to work together. Bishop, I would make you my second in command."

Silhouette, for years a loyal toady, didn't like the sound of this. "Second?" he cried. "There is only room for one second in command, and that is me!"

"Silhouette, control your temper!" Onyx boomed, his eyes glowing a fiery red. Mandy gasped.

"What about my friends?" Bishop asked.

"They can assist us as well, dear boy. But you are the one I am interested in working with. Together, we could control everything...for the betterment of everyone, of course. I assure you that I only want what is best."

"Bull," Gary blasted. "You're full of it!"

"Silence, large one! Now, nephew, what is your decision?"

"Can I have a few minutes with my friends to talk about this?"

"Of course. I've waited this long. A few minutes more mean nothing."

Rising from the throne, Onyx walked down the steps, past Bishop and out a door that opened as he approached it. A few shadowy figures scurried behind him.

Bishop turned to his friends. "I don't know how much time we've got. I'm not even sure whether or not this place is bugged. So we've got to speak quickly and quietly."

Justin was indignant. "If this character is your uncle, Bishop, then you'd better get him to let me go!"

"Are you afraid, Justin?" Gary asked.

"A Wellington is afraid of nothing! I just don't have time for all this foolishness!"

"How do I tell him that I don't want to join him and still get us out of here?" Bishop asked. "Anybody have any ideas? I'm open for suggestions."

"I say that you blow him off," Gary said. "Tell him that you'll get back to him and then forget about it. He's your uncle. What's he gonna do? Kill you? He needs you."

Onyx returned to the room. "Well, nephew, I trust you have made the correct decision by now."

Bishop took a deep breath. "We've decided that the best thing for me to do is to think about it for a couple of days."

"Do not play games with me! I would much prefer you be on my side. However, if you choose to fight against me, then you and I will be at war. You may depart from here for now. The next time we meet, you won't find me so forgiving! I don't make idle threats!" Onyx waved his hand and the fires in the room instantly went out.

The next thing Bishop and his friends knew, they were back in Bishop's living room. They were lying on the floor, as if awakening from a nap.

"Boy, your uncle sure gets ticked off easily," Gary said.

Justin was dazed. "Uhhh…What happened?"

"Wow! It's like one minute we were somewhere else and the next we're back," Mandy said, stating the obvious.

Bishop spoke quietly. "I don't think this mess is going to get any easier from here on."

"Speaking of messes, check him out," Gary said as he pointed to Justin, who was lying on top of the birthday cake.

"My cake!" Justin cried.

Gary chuckled. "It's Bish's cake, not yours."

"If any of you want to stay behind, I don't blame you," Bishop said. "But as for me, my father started this, and I guess it's up to me to finish it. I'd better make sure nothing's been broken or messed up around here. My grandfather will be back soon." Bishop walked into the kitchen, inspecting various furnishings along the way.

Gary raced after Bishop. "Wait up! I'll help you."

"Me, too," Mandy said. She also left the room.

Justin sat up. He frowned as tried to clean the cake off his pants. "Alone again, naturally," he sighed.

Suddenly, someone grabbed Justin by the back of his collar and yanked him off the floor. A second later he was looking face to face with Onyx, who was holding him in the air by the scruff of his neck. Justin was frozen with fear.

"I sense great potential in you, boy," Onyx hissed.

"Me?" Justin squeaked.

Onyx produced an object that looked like an expensive pen. "I need you to follow your friends everywhere they go. I want you to carry this tracking device, designed to look like a pen. It will allow me to keep track of Bishop, through you." Onyx inserted the pen into Justin's shirt pocket. "If you need to contact me, just click the pen three times in succession, and I will be there."

Justin tried to sound brave. "Why should I do anything for you? I don't even know you!"

"First, if you do as I ask, then when we are done, I will grant you your greatest wish. Anything you want will be yours."

"I already have everything I want!" Justin scoffed. "I'm a Wellington!"

"You do not have extraordinary abilities like Bishop," Onyx growled. "Join me and I will see to it that you also have a special power. Any power you desire. What will it be, boy. Flying? Invisibility? Super strength? Name the power and it can be yours."

Justin was tempted by the offer. Ever since he discovered that Bishop had special powers, he felt that he might lose Mandy to his rival. But his father had always told him to never accept anyone's first offer. "Get as much as you can from a deal" was one of his father's favorite sayings.

"Maybe," Justin said. "What else can you offer?"

Onyx closed his hand around Justin's throat.

"If you do as I ask, then I shall also let you live!" Onyx dropped Justin. He crashed to the floor, sitting directly on the remains of the cake. And then, Onyx was gone. The others returned to the room a few moments later. Bishop was now wearing his uniform.

Gary looked at Justin and laughed. "Hey, Wellington, didn't your mother ever tell you not to play with your food?"

"I tripped, that's all." Justin eyes Bishop's uniform. "Uh, nice duds, Chance. Not!"

Mandy was quick to defend Bishop's new look. "I like the uniform, Bishop. You look very handsome."

"I do?" Bishop asked.

"He does?" Justin croaked.

"Yes, he does," Mandy smiled.

"Fine," Justin said. "Okay, so, when do we leave?"

"Why do you want to come?" Gary asked. "You don't even like us!"

"I have my reasons."

"Yeah, you don't trust Mandy alone with Bish," Gary said as the doorbell rang.

Bishop opened the door to Miss Mann. The sight of Bishop in the uniform momentarily stunned her.

"My goodness! The last person I saw wearing that was...was..."

"My father?"

"Yes."

"It fit him?"

"Oh yes. The material adjusts itself to fit the wearer."

"I don't know about this," Bishop frowned. "I look like a superhero or something."

"You are a hero, Bishop. That is your destiny."

Mandy stepped forward. "Miss Mann, we've seen Onyx," she said.

Miss Mann was stunned. "What? He's been here?"

"Not exactly," Bishop explained. "He kidnapped us and brought us to his...his..."

"His throne room!" Justin exclaimed.

"It was a real dump!" Gary added.

Miss Mann looked unnerved. Why would Onyx suddenly make himself known after hiding for so many years?

"He knows all about our quest," Bishop said.

Miss Mann took a deep breath. She then produced an envelope from her pocket. "Take this, but don't open it until you've reached your first destination," she said, handing the envelope to Bishop. She then faced the group. "Okay, everyone! You don't have much time! Now that he is out of hiding, Onyx will be coming after you again."

"Before we go, we need to figure out what to tell our parents," Mandy said. "We should at least leave messages for them."

"I will take care of that," Miss Mann declared. "I shall now use my power so that you will be free to begin."

Gary eyed his chocolate-covered nemesis. "Maybe you could use your power to clean up Justin."

"Quiet! This requires concentration." Miss Mann placed her hands to her head, closed her eyes and started to hum. Four puffs of smoke materialized out of thin air and quickly formed into recognizable shapes: Exact duplicates of Bishop, Mandy, Gary and Justin.

Miss Mann exhaled. "It's been a long time since I've had to do that. I hope I've done it right."

Justin stepped forward and poked his duplicate in the chest. The duplicate poked Justin back with great force. "Ow!" Justin cried. "What's going on here?"

"I have created exact duplicates of all of you," Miss Mann explained. "They will stay behind and take your places so that no one will know you are gone. Your duplicates will do everything that you would normally do."

"Don't we need to train them or something?" Gary asked.

"No," Miss Mann replied. "They are good to go. I hope."

Bishop inspected his duplicate. "What do we do now?"

"You must begin your quest," Miss Mann said. "And I must go."

Mandy was surprised at how fast everything was moving along. "Do you have to leave so soon?"

"Yes, I do. You can find your next clue, and one of our operatives, in the city of brotherly love. Goodbye, my friends, and good luck."

At that, Miss Mann dashed out the front door, followed by the duplicates of Gary, Mandy and Justin. The Bishop duplicate stayed behind.

"I'm going to your room to start your homework," Duplicate Bishop said as he headed upstairs.

"Hey, I could get used to that," Gary smiled.

An uncertain Bishop attempted to take command. "Miss Mann said that we should start in the city of brotherly love. That's Philadelphia. I'll call a taxi to get us to the airport."

"A taxi?" Justin sniffed. "I'm not taking a taxi. I'll call our chauffer and he'll bring the limo. That's how my family travels."

"Fine," Bishop said. "You'd better go upstairs and clean up. You can borrow some of my clothes."

"I'm not gonna wear your stuff."

"You'd rather walk around with cake on your butt?" Gary sneered. "Come on, Justin, you're wasting time. Move it!" Justin hurried upstairs.

"What about us?" Mandy asked. "Should we go pack or something?"

"There's no time," Bishop said. "We'll buy whatever we need on the way. You sure you guys are up for this?"

Gary stepped forward as if reporting for duty. "Ab-so-lutely."

Mandy smiled. "We're with you, Bishop."


The doorbell rang about fifteen minutes later. Bishop was taken aback when he answered the door. Parked in front of his house was the longest car he had ever seen. It was jet black with a satellite dish attached to the trunk. A man in a blue three-piece suit stood at the front door.

"Is Master Wellington here?" he asked.

Justin came to the door. Instead of his normal preppy clothing, he was wearing a plain shirt and jeans, and he looked very distressed.

"It's about time you got here," Justin said.

"Justin," Mandy protested, "that's no way to talk to another person."

"He's just an employee. C'mon."

Justin walked out of the house. Bishop, Mandy and Gary followed. Bishop looked up as he locked the door. His duplicate was staring down at him from his bedroom window. Bishop ran to the limo. He still was not used to seeing another person who looked exactly like him.

Once they were all inside the car, Justin tried to impress Mandy by showing her all of its expensive extras. They included three flat screen televisions and several laptops.

"So," Gary asked, "what airline are we going to fly?"

Justin pulled a cell phone from his pants pocket. "A Wellington doesn't travel by commercial airline. I'll call my father. I'm sure we can use his jet."

Justin punched the number and waited. "Hello. Justin here. Let me speak to my father." Justin looked at his companions. "I got his secretary."

Justin's tone turned to one of anger. "Fine, if he's not there, then patch me through to my mother." There was a short pause. Justin frowned. "She's at the spa? Can't you page her? It's important! Tell her it's her son." After another brief pause Justin said to his friends, "My mother's, uh, busy and can't be disturbed."

Mandy looked at Justin. She felt sorry for him. She knew that her parents would always take her phone call if she needed them. "It's okay, Justin, we'll just take a regular plane."

Justin shook his head. "No, I'll handle it." He spoke again into the phone. "I'm headed to the airport and I need to use the jet. Call ahead and arrange it," he barked.

The limo driver soon dropped Justin and the others outside a bustling airport terminal. They hurried inside.

"We'll need some spending money," Justin said. "I'll hit an ATM." Justin walked to a cash machine with the others close behind. "The stupid bank only lets you take out a maximum of $400 a day, but that should hold us for awhile."

"Isn't that stupid bank Wellington Bank and Trust?" Gary asked. "Owned by your family?"

"Yeah, but that's not what I meant," Justin said, embarrassed. "What I meant was…" Justin was interrupted by a noise from the ATM, which began dispensing twenty-dollar bills. "Chump change," Justin sniffed.

Bishop stepped up to the machine. "I think I'll get some money too. Hey Gary, how much do you think we'll need?"

"Oh, I don't know," Gary smiled. "Three grand or so?"

Justin laughed as Bishop started pressing the buttons on the machine. "Uh, hello? Anybody home? You can't get money from the machine without a card. And I already told you the most you can get is $400."

Once again, Justin was silenced by a noise from the cash machine. This time it began spewing bills with such speed that Bishop couldn't grab them all. Passersby took note of all the cash flying about.

Bishop struggled to grab as much cash as he could. "It's too fast. I haven't gotten complete control yet. Hey guys, help me pick this stuff up before everyone else does."

Justin was dumbfounded. "This is impossible!"

"Bish can do things that you can't, no matter how much money you have," Gary said.

Mandy was troubled. "Bishop, you're taking an awful lot of money. Isn't this stealing?"

Gary answered for his flustered friend. "Give him a break, Mandy. He's trying to be a hero here."

Bishop smiled. "Besides, it isn't stealing. I took it from Justin's account."

"What?" Justin cried.

"Hey, I'm trying to save a world here. It's just chump change, right? You won't miss it."

The four friends headed towards the gate where the Wellington jet was docked. An attractive blonde flight attendant with sparkling blue eyes was waiting for them at the door.

As the four passed by her, no one noticed Bishop's ring, which had turned black. The flight attendant watched as they boarded the plane. Her blue eyes were now glowing a fiery red.

# Chapter 4

## Out of the Frying Pan and Into the Fire

Bishop had never flown before, but he had seen several movies that took place on airplanes and the Wellington aircraft looked nothing like any of the planes in those films. Instead of many rows of tight, cramped seats, this plane, known as the Wellington Wing, had plush chairs and a long sofa along one side of the cabin. There were a few tables scattered around and in the front and back of the plane there were large screen televisions mounted on each wall.

Bishop's moment of awe ended abruptly when someone shoved him from behind. It was Justin.

"Come on, Chance, move already," Justin commanded. "We haven't got all day." Clearly Justin was indifferent to such luxury.

Bishop sat on the sofa. Mandy joined him. Gary walked over to a wooden cabinet under one of the windows.

"Cool, this must be the liquor cabinet." Gary tried unsuccessfully to open it. "Hey, it won't budge!"

"Of course not," Justin sniffed. "It's locked. Do you think my father would let everyone get at his good liquor?"

"I don't want liquor. I want a cold soda," Gary grumbled as he flopped down in front of one of the television sets.

Within seconds, a tall, twenty-something flight attendant with short, spiked black hair and sharp facial features was at Gary's side.

"My name is Erik," he said. "Welcome aboard, Mr. Wellington. I'll get your soda right away."

"Yo, Erik," Justin said from across the cabin. "I'm Mr. Wellington, not him."

Erik walked over to Justin. "I'm so sorry, sir. I'm new here."

Justin shuddered at the thought that anyone could mistake Gary for him. "That's obvious."

"We should be taking off for Philadelphia in a few minutes, so you should all buckle up. And in case of an emergency water landing..."

Justin rudely interrupted. "O'Leary can be used as a flotation device," he laughed.

"Jerk," Gary grumbled.

"Okay, I'll be back after we've taken off." Erik turned and walked to the front of the plane.

"He's irritating," Justin sniffed. "I'll have to talk to my father about replacing him."

"I can't believe we're going to Philadelphia," Gary said as he looked around. "I've never gone that far from home before without my folks." Gary studied the television screen in front of him. "Hey, where's the remote for this set?"

"It's built into the arm of the seat," Justin answered. "But you can't turn it on until we've taken off. It interferes with the plane's instruments. Sheesh, don't you know anything?"

Erik returned after the plane had taken off. He approached Gary, who was busy channel surfing.

"Okay, big guy, what can I get you?"

Justin interrupted Erik once again. "Mineral water!"

"Wait your turn, prep," Gary said.

"It's my plane, O'Leary," Justin growled. "I'll order first."

Mandy tried to keep the peace. "Could you bring us three sodas and one mineral water?"

"Absolutely," Erik bowed. "Say, how would you all like to see the cockpit? Captain Marshan enjoys showing people how the plane operates."

"I've already seen the cockpit," Justin sighed. "Many times."

"I haven't," Bishop said. "That would be great."

Erik moved toward the front of the plane. "I'll check with the captain."

Gary was enthusiastic. "Bish! Dude! The cockpit! How cool is that?"

"I doubt there'd be room for you in there, O'Leary," Justin said. "Maybe we should have taken a jumbo jet."

"Yeah, and maybe you could ride in the baggage compartment," Gary shot back.

"The pilot said it would be all right for you all to come up," Erik called from the front of the plane. "Follow me."

"Hey, what about my water?" Justin complained.

Everybody ignored him as they moved toward the cockpit. Bishop tentatively looked inside and was awestruck by all the controls and lights around him. He glanced at the pilot, who looked just like all the pilots he had ever seen before in the movies. Sitting next to him at the other set of controls was the co-pilot.

The pilot smiled as he turned around in his seat. "Hey kids! Come right in and take a look around."

"Can we all fit?" Mandy asked. Justin looked at Gary, as if readying another snide remark about his size.

"Shut your pie hole, Justin," Gary warned.

"I didn't say anything," Justin replied with obvious false innocence.

Everybody was so dazzled by the complexities of the cockpit controls that nobody noticed Bishop's ring. It was glowing black.

Bishop held out his hand to the pilot. "Hi, my name is...."

The pilot took his hand and shook it. "Bishop Chance, right? I'm Captain Marshan."

Bishop was immediately suspicious. "You know my name?" he asked.

"Of course. I know that you are Bishop, and you are here with Gary O'Leary, Mandy Conway and Justin Wellington III." Marshan turned toward Justin. "You know, I'm not used to flying with royalty, Mr. Wellington."

Justin smiled. He loved this type of flattery.

"How did you know our names?" Bishop asked.

"Under normal circumstances, the pilots on private planes always know the names of their passengers." Marshan's smile widened. "But there's nothing normal about these circumstances."

"What does that mean?" Bishop asked, his voice betraying his sudden nervousness.

"The truth is that an uncle of yours told me to look you up. This is as far up as I could get." Marshan laughed. The co-pilot also chuckled.

"Onyx sent you?" Bishop yelped.

Mandy suddenly noticed Bishop's ring. "Bishop!" she gasped. "Look!"

Bishop and the others stared at the ring, now glowing a menacing black. Justin panicked. "I'm outta here!" he said as he turned toward the door, seeking an escape from the cockpit. Mandy turned with Justin. The two found themselves face to face with Erik, whose face suddenly morphed into something quite monstrous, complete with glowing red eyes and a ghastly oversized mouth brimming with razor sharp teeth. Justin and Mandy both screamed. The creature formally known as Erik blocked the door.

"We took the place of the real pilot and co-pilot," Marshan explained. "And, as you can see, the flight attendant."

"You mean you killed them?" Gary croaked.

"Don't be ridiculous. We simply tied them up and locked them in a car trunk. Someone will find them. Someday. Hee hee hee."

"What do you intend to do?" Justin asked, somewhat sheepishly. "Kill us?"

"Oh, we're not going to lay a finger on any of you." Marshan smiled again. "We plan on leaving you right here while we teleport somewhere safe and watch the plane crash."

"Teleport?" Gary gasped. "Like on Star Trek?"

"Yes. It's my special power. I can teleport small groups of people."

"Then you have to take us with you!" Mandy was loud.

Marshan laughed an awful, raspy laugh. "You just don't get it, do you, little miss?"

"Yeah," the Erik thing sneered. "Borrow a buck from young Wellington here and buy a clue."

The pilot grinned at them. A shiver ran down Bishop's spine. "Any last words that you would like me to convey to Onyx?"

"You can tell him that he's not going to get away with this!" Gary said with surprising defiance. Then he turned to Bishop. "Uh, right, Bish?"

"Nothing personal, kids, but we've got to go," Marshan pushed the steering wheel forward. The plane began to tip earthward.

"What are you doing?" Justin shrieked.

Marshan chuckled. "Isn't it obvious? Good-bye, and bad luck." Seconds later, both pilots and the flight attendant simply dematerialized. Bishop and his friends were alone in the cockpit.

Mandy grabbed Bishop's arm. "What are we going to do? Can you fly this plane?"

"I don't know, I've never been in a plane before."

Gary looked out the front window. The plane was still in descent and had broken through the cloud cover. "Dude, you've got to do something, or we're dead!" he cried. "Use your power!"

Beads of sweat appeared on Bishop's forehead. "I don't know if my power can handle an entire airplane! Does anyone have any other ideas?"

"I'm gonna puke!" Justin stated in a calm, matter-of-fact manner. "I am so going to puke.

"That's real constructive," Gary snapped.

"Wait a minute!" Bishop said. "I saw a movie about this once," He reached over and strapped on a face microphone. "The person left flying the plane sat in the pilot's chair and put the headphones on so he could hear the control tower."

Bishop switched on a speaker. "Hello! Hello! Can anyone hear me? We're in trouble here!"

A voice came through the headphones. "This is Philadelphia Airport. Who is this?"

"My name is Bishop. I'm on a private plane. The pilot and co-pilot are both—um—well, they can't come to the phone right now. And I'm flying the plane."

"What?" the voice replied. "Who is this really? Is this some sort of a joke?" Bishop then heard the voice say to someone else, "Hey, Greg, it sounds like a kid on the radio."

"I am a kid!" Bishop screamed, his voice betraying his nervousness. "There is nobody left on this plane who knows how to land it! I need help! And we're descending very quickly. I need help!"

"Yeah. Help! Help!!" Justin cried.

Bishop could hear Greg in the background. "This is the real deal, Ralph. This transmission is really coming from a private plane."

Ralph took control. "All right kid, don't worry. We'll talk you down. Now listen to me and pay attention. Do exactly as I say, and you should be able to land that plane. You are approaching Philadelphia Airport. First, put your hands on the wheel."

"Okay," Bishop said, reaching forward. "Done."

"Slowly pull back on the wheel. That will ease your descent. While you do that, I'm going to alert the ground crew to get ready for an emergency landing."

"An emergency landing?" Justin squeaked. "That means we're going to crash! My father's going to kill me if I crash his plane."

"It will be a little late for that," Gary said, trying to sound caustic, but simply sounded scared. "Bish, you really should use your power on the plane. Now!"

"Okay! Okay! I'll try!" Bishop kept his hands on the wheel as he spoke to the control panel. "Plane, slow down and start a gradual descent to the ground. Do whatever you have to do to land this plane safely."

"This is never going to work," Justin moaned. "I really am going to barf."

Ralph's voice returned. "I can see you on the radar now, Bishop. Turn on your landing gear and head for landing strip number 8." Bishop then heard Ralph say, "This kid is smooth, Greg. He's talkin' to the plane the way I talk to my car!"

"Now, plane, lower the landing gear and head for landing strip number 8," Bishop said, wiping the sweat from his forehead. There was a loud noise from below them.

Mandy jumped. "What was that?"

Bishop tried to reassure her. "Probably just the landing gear," he said.

The voice in Bishop's headset returned. "Your descent is fine. Actually, it's remarkable. Start applying the brakes and remember to keep it steady. You sure you've never done this before, kid?"

"Yes, I'm sure. All right, plane, just keep us steady." Bishop was now in full sweat. Mandy looked very worried. Justin was looking rather green. Gary was clutching a lollipop in both hands.

Justin closed his eyes as the small plane touched down on the runway.

"You did it, Bish!" Gary screamed, slapping his buddy on the back. "You did it!" Bishop was too preoccupied to notice.

"Alright, plane, apply the brakes. Slowly!"

Mandy leaned over and kissed Bishop on his cheek. "My hero!" she cheered. Bishop smiled.

Gary turned toward Justin. "So, smart aleck, what do you say now?"

Justin wasn't standing where he had been moments ago. Gary looked down at the floor. Justin had passed out.

"At least he didn't puke!" Gary said. The sound of Justin vomiting on the floor followed. "Oh, gross," Gary groaned, stepping back from the mess. "Way to go, champ."

"Very good, young man," Ralph said to Bishop over the headset. "A professional couldn't have brought her down any better. When you get off the plane I'd like to shake your hand."

"Thank you, sir." Bishop switched off the microphone.

Now that he was beginning to recover from the sheer panic of having to land the plane, Bishop fully realized the situation he was in. How in the world could he explain what had happened? To where had the crew disappeared? And why were four teenagers in the cockpit, landing the plane? There was only one answer: Flee! And fast!

Bishop took command. "The minute the plane stops, and the cabin is depressurized, we're getting out of here. I don't want to have to explain this to anybody." He then addressed the control panel one last time. "Please erase everything that happened from the black box and other flight recordings that are on board."

Once the plane was at the terminal, Bishop opened the door to a crowd of airport personnel that had assembled to meet him. "The fellow you want is in the cockpit," he told the group. "He saved us all." Bishop was a convincing liar. As the crowd moved forward, Bishop and his friends were able to slip past them and enter the terminal, where they did their best to blend in with other travelers. Gary and Bishop were helping a wobbly Justin.

"I can't believe there are no reporters here," Mandy said. "I would have guessed that someone in the control tower would have tipped off the press about this." Mandy then froze. Across the terminal she saw a crowd of reporters armed with cameras and microphones. Bishop and Gary also froze, releasing Justin.

"Quick! Go that way!" Bishop pointed to the left. Bishop and Gary turned. Justin, on the other hand, collapsed to the floor.

"Get him up! I'll get a cab," Mandy said as she ran ahead.

Bishop and Gary picked Justin up and continued holding him as they rushed out of the terminal.

The four friends were soon crushed in the back seat of a taxi. Bishop reached into his jacket pocket and produced the envelope Miss Mann had given him earlier.

"I guess it's time to open this," he said. Bishop quickly read the letter to himself, then aloud. "It says we need to find a bell where a bell shouldn't be."

"Can't anybody just give a straight answer anymore?" Justin groaned. He was feeling queasy, and the cab ride wasn't helping. "What's with all the riddles?"

The taxi driver turned and looked at them. Nervously, Bishop thrust his right hand at the driver, who flinched. False alarm. Bishop's ring remained white.

"Whew!" Gary loudly exhaled. The driver mumbled something insulting under his breath, his eyes returning to the road.

"Before we go looking for any bells, we better get to a hotel," Bishop said.

"Take us to the best hotel in town," Justin barked at the taxi driver. Even when nauseous, he was still a Wellington.

The driver dropped Bishop and his friends at the most expensive hotel in the city. As they entered the spacious lobby they noticed many uniformed staffers bustling about, hurriedly tending to the needs of the privileged.

Mandy frowned. "This looks very expensive. Can we afford it?"

"Don't worry." Bishop was cool. "Remember, money is no object."

"That's always been my motto," Justin boasted.

Bishop approached one of the many hotel clerks stationed behind a long marble counter. "I would like the best suite you have. With at least two bedrooms."

"Uh, I think I'll take my own suite," Justin added.

"No way. We're sticking together." Bishop once again took command. "One suite, please."

"We require an adult's approval before renting to young people such as yourselves," the clerk explained.

Bishop was quick with his response. "Mr. Justin Wellington Jr. has already authorized us," he said, reaching over the counter to lightly touch the clerk's computer. Sure enough, Justin's father's name and an authorization code appeared on the monitor.

"Very good, young sir. I see authorization for four young people under the name of Wellington. However there is nothing here about payment. How did you wish to pay for that?"

Bishop pulled a large wad of cash out of his jacket pocket and set it on the counter.

"Yes, sir!" the clerk chirped.

Before long, Bishop, Mandy and Gary were admiring their suite. Large windows afforded panoramic views of Philadelphia at sunset. Justin was less impressed, simply because he was used to such splendor.

Mandy gazed at the orange and pink horizon. "What happens now, Bishop?"

"It's getting dark. We'll look for the bell tomorrow. I'm going down to the hotel pool for a swim."

"You need all the practice you can get," Justin said. He never missed a chance to criticize Bishop's swimming.

Bishop frowned at Justin, then turned and faced Mandy. "I need to pick up a bathing suit and some other things at one of the stores downstairs."

"I'll stay here and order some food from room service," Gary said. "Money is no object, right?" He was perpetually hungry.

"How do your parents pay your food bills?" Justin asked Gary. "Your appetite would bankrupt *my* family!"

Mandy was at Bishop's side. "I'm going to go look through the shops in the lobby," she said.

"I'll go with you," Justin offered.

Mandy smiled. "Those would be dress shops, Justin."

The thought of spending an hour looking at women's clothes didn't appeal to Justin. "What am I supposed to do?" he asked. "Stay here and watch O'Leary eat us all into the poor house?"

"Looks that way," Bishop replied. "Unless you want to take a dip."

"No way," Justin sneered. "I hate public pools."

"More than you hate me?" Gary asked.

"Good point." Justin followed Bishop and Mandy out the door.

Bishop and Justin entered the poolroom from the men's locker room. They were both wearing swimsuits. There was only one other person in the room: a boy about their age. He had short bright red hair and was wearing a black swimsuit with a red stripe running through it. The boy dove off the diving board as Bishop and Justin entered, surfacing near them.

"That was great. How long have you been diving?" Bishop asked the boy. Justin ignored them both and walked over to the diving board.

"A few years at least. I've lost track," the boy replied. "I haven't seen you around before."

"I just checked in with my friends," Bishop said. "We're here for a couple of days. How long are you staying?"

"I'm not a guest. I live close by. I have a friend who works here and lets me use the pool when there aren't a lot of people in it. Tourists don't spend a lot of time in the pool. They're too busy sight-seeing."

"That's us," Bishop smiled. "Tourists! We want to see everything."

"If you're looking for landmarks, you should check out the Liberty Bell. It's downtown, near Constitution Hall. It's in a small glass building, about the size of a large room. You can't miss it."

Bishop realized at that moment that the Liberty Bell must be the bell referred to in his clue. "Of course!" he exclaimed. "The Liberty Bell!"

"What about it?" the boy asked.

Bishop fumbled, not wanting to reveal information about his quest to a stranger. "Nothing. It's just that I forgot all about the Liberty Bell. Uh, thanks. We'll check it out tomorrow."

The boy watched as Bishop jumped into the pool and swam to the far end.

"See you there, Bishop," the boy muttered to himself.

Bishop reached the other end of the pool, where he found Justin floating with his feet resting on the edge. "Who's your friend?" Justin asked.

"I didn't get his name." Bishop turned around and looked back across the pool.

There was no sign of the boy.

# Chapter 5

## You Can Ring My Bell

Bright and early the following morning, Bishop and his friends approached the small glass building that was home to the Liberty Bell.

"Everything looks so normal," Mandy sighed. "It's hard to believe we're doing what we're doing, isn't it?"

Justin was fretful. "I keep expecting Onyx to appear from out of nowhere and cut our heads off or something."

"In your case, that would be an improvement," Gary said.

Mandy paused near a sign. "This sign says that this place doesn't open for another two hours."

"Great," Justin grumbled to Bishop. "You made us all rush over here at the crack of dawn and we can't even get in!"

Suddenly, the boy from the hotel pool appeared from around the corner of the building. He was wearing a black uniform with a red stripe running through it, just like his swimsuit the night before.

"We meet again," the boy said.

"Hi," Bishop answered.

"You're the kid from the pool," Justin said with limited interest.

"That's right, Justin."

"How did you know my name?"

"Everybody knows Justin Wellington III," the boy replied. Justin couldn't help smiling, but Bishop felt strangely apprehensive. "In fact, I know all your names," the boy continued. "You can call me Print."

"Print? That's an odd name," Bishop said.

"You should talk, Bishop," Print countered.

Justin laughed. "He's got you there, Chance."

"I'm here to help you with your current clue."

Gary was suspicious. "How do you know about the clues?"

"I'm one of Alabaster's agents," Print explained. "Christie Rae Mann sent me."

"You knew my father?" Bishop gasped.

Print shook his head. "No, I was just a little kid when your parents died. My parents were his agents, and I took over their job when they died. But my father knew your father well and he said he was a prince."

"I thought Miss Mann said he was a king," Justin remarked.

"He meant he was a great man."

"We're pretty sure our latest clue has to do with the Liberty Bell," Bishop said. "But we can't get inside for another two hours."

Print smiled. "No problem. I'll just use my power to get us in there. I can change into any fictional character from any book." Print suddenly morphed into a muscular man with long red hair wearing an animal skin around his waist. Bishop and his friends were speechless. "I think the body of Hercules, the strongest man in history, should get us in there," Print-Hercules declared. "But before I open the door, you need to deactivate the security system, Bishop. This will reduce the risk of getting caught and attracting attention."

Gary stepped forward. "Uh, you're wearing a loincloth and you're worried about attracting attention?"

Bishop placed one hand on the security panel and deactivated it. Print-Hercules then ripped the door from its frame. The five adventurers entered the building.

Bishop was worried. "We'd better hurry and find our next clue. I don't know how long we can stand around here unnoticed. Check the bell, inside and out."

Print morphed back to his true form. Bishop and his friends could only stare. "Why don't you send Gary outside?" Print suggested. "He can make sure we're not disturbed."

"You okay with that?" Bishop asked Gary.

"Sure. I could use some fresh air...away from Justin!" Gary left the building as the others began looking around. After ten minutes of searching the room and the bell from top to bottom without discovering anything useful or unusual, they all looked discouraged. "We've done everything but ring the stupid thing," Justin sighed.

"Hey! You could be onto something, Justin," Bishop said. "Maybe, if we ring it, something will happen."

"I remember reading that they are so afraid of the bell cracking anymore than it already is, that they haven't rung it for over twenty years," Mandy recalled. "Be careful."

Bishop slid under the bell and reached up into it. A bong was heard. And then a holographic image of Alabaster appeared.

"Bishop! It's your father!" Mandy gasped.

"He'd better give us a better clue than last time," Justin complained.

Alabaster's image began to speak. "I hope that you have gotten this far unharmed, my son. In order to find your next clue, you must locate the right keys. You will find them to the South. Remember not to wreck your chances by making the wrong decision. Goodbye, Bishop." With that, Alabaster was gone again.

"Bye, dad," Bishop whispered under his breath. He was still moved by these unexpected images of his father. Everyone was quiet for a few moments.

Justin broke the silence. "Now what the heck does that mean?"

"I guess our biggest problem right now is to figure out this new clue," Bishop said.

"Wrong!" a voice boomed from behind them.

Gary was standing at the doorway with someone who was dressed very similarly to Print, except that he was wearing a white uniform with a blue stripe running through it.

"Your biggest problem right now is that you have a traitor in your midst!" the stranger declared.

If his friends had been looking at him at that moment, they would have noticed that Justin had turned white as a sheet. Who had found him out? Who knew he was spying for Onyx? Who was this new person who had just walked in with Gary?

Before Bishop could respond, Print confronted his accuser. "Well, it didn't take you long to track me down this time, brother," he said.

"You two are brothers?" Mandy asked.

Print scowled. "Yes. His name is Reprint. Isn't that clever?"

"I am one of Alabaster's operatives," Reprint declared. "Print, here, is the traitor. He works for Onyx."

Print began to morph again. "Yes, and you're too late!" he hissed. "I already have the clue, and I'm going to tell Onyx everything! He'll reach the next clue before any of you do!" Print completed his transformation. Standing in his place was an exact duplicate of the pirate Captain Hook. "If anyone wishes to stop me, I have a sword and a hook with their name on it! So, if you don't mind, I'll take my leave."

Reprint also began to morph. "Not yet, bro," he said. "You're not going anywhere." Within seconds, Reprint transformed himself into a duplicate of Peter Pan.

"I share the same power as my brother," Reprint-Pan said to the others. "It must be in our genes."

Print-Hook tried several times to stab Reprint-Pan with his sword, but Reprint-Pan always flew out of the way. Reprint-Pan kept trying to grab Print-Hook and hoist him into the air, but Print-Hook always dodged. Print-Hook finally managed to injure his brother, slicing his foot with his sword. Momentarily blinded by pain, Reprint-Pan flew too high too quickly, slamming head first into the ceiling. He instantly morphed back to his normal form and fell unconscious to the floor. Print-Hook stood over him.

"Well, brother, I believe that I finally have the upper hand," Print-Hook laughed. "Or is that the upper hook? It's a shame that you are not conscious to appreciate the last few seconds of life you have left. I bid you a fond farewell." But before Print-Hook could finish off his brother, Bishop lunged and tackled him to the floor.

Print-Hook was enraged. "My quarrel is not with you, Bishop! Take your friends and get out of here! This is between my brother and me!"

"Sorry, Print. I won't let you harm him." Bishop sprang to his feet, produced the dagger Miss Mann had given him and thrust it toward Print-Hook.

"Do you think that small dagger is any threat to me?" Print-Hook sneered. "I'm warning you for the last time, take your friends and get out of here."

Justin knew an opening line when he heard one. "You heard him, Mandy. Let's go!"

"No! We can't leave Bishop alone," Mandy cried.

Justin wasted no time in dragging an unwilling Mandy safely out of the room.

Inside, Bishop and Print-Hook circled each other, with Bishop repeatedly dodging Print-Hook's sword and hook. Print-Hook surprised him with a kick to the stomach and knocked Bishop to the floor. Print-Hook moved in for the kill, but suddenly an object struck him in the head. He was distracted, but not hurt.

"What was that?" Print-Hook howled. He glanced toward the floor and saw a miniature replica of the Liberty Bell at his feet. His eyes then moved to Gary, who was clutching another miniature bell. "A souvenir?" Print-Hook hissed. "You threw a cheap souvenir at me?"

"Get him, Bish!" Gary cheered.

Gary's distraction worked. Bishop leaped at Print-Hook and knocked the sword out of his hand with his dagger. The sword crashed to the ground along with several of Print-Hook's fingers. Print-Hook screamed. Unable to keep his concentration, he changed back to his normal form. Print's screaming awakened Reprint.

Bishop was horrified. He had maimed another human being. "I'm sorry! It's the first time I've used this dagger in combat! I didn't mean to hurt you!"

"I'll get you for this!" Print screamed.

Reprint opened his eyes and looked around. He saw his brother crouched on the floor, his uniform covered with blood. "I'd better get you to a doctor, brother. Fast."

Gary couldn't believe his ears. "He tried to kill you just a few minutes ago!" he exclaimed.

"I know," Reprint said as he calmly helped his brother to his feet. "But if I left him here, I would be no better than him. I fight only when necessary, and then, never to kill. So I will take him with me and see that he receives care."

"But he lost some fingers!" Mandy gasped.

"They'll grow back in time. Any injuries we receive while in changed form heal themselves eventually after we change back. You had better be going. This place will be opening shortly and people are going to start coming and asking questions." He changed once again to Peter Pan and lifted his brother up into the air. "I'll meet up with you later, Bishop."

With that, Reprint-Pan and Print were gone.

"My goodness, people come and go so quickly around here," Mandy said.

Bishop was worried. "I think it would be best if we followed their example and left as quickly as possible."

"There's one thing I don't understand, Bish," Gary said. "Why didn't your ring warn you about Print in the first place?"

"The truth is that I forgot to look at it." Bishop eyed his ring and frowned. "That's odd. It's still glowing black."

"Maybe it got damaged in the battle," a nervous Justin offered. He knew the ring was glowing because of him.

"Maybe it just hates you, Justin!" Gary remarked.

"What?" Justin croaked. Was Gary onto him?

"Chill, man. It was a joke!"

"Where are we going now?" Mandy asked.

Bishop looked lost. "My father said we would find our next clue in the south."

"He also said something about locating the right keys," Gary recalled. "What's up with that?"

Justin was suddenly helpful. "There's a place around the bottom tip of Florida called the Florida Keys. My family goes scuba diving there every year."

Mandy turned to Bishop. "Scuba! That's it! Didn't your father say something like you shouldn't wreck your chances by making the wrong decision? Maybe he's trying to tell you that the next clue is hidden in one of the shipwrecks near the Florida Keys. People are always diving there, looking for lost treasure!"

Bishop smiled. "Good thought, Mandy. Okay, everyone. Let's get out of here. We're going south!"

"Do we have to fly?" Justin asked. "I mean, Onyx could send another killer pilot, or…"

"Don't worry about that," Bishop interrupted. "Now that he knows I can fly a plane if I have to, I don't think Onyx will waste his time."

Bishop looked around the room. "Whatever any of you do, don't say where we're going out loud. We don't know who might be listening."

Justin nervously glanced at Bishop's ring. It was still glowing black.

# Chapter 6

## Just in Case

While the original Justin was on his way to Florida, his duplicate was enjoying the good life back home. He was dressed in expensive white tennis clothes and had just hit a perfect serve on one of the large outdoor tennis courts at the palatial Wellington country club. Duplicate Bishop, who was similarly attired, swung at the air in an unsuccessful attempt to return the serve.

"Beat you again, Chance," Duplicate Justin said. "You're just as bad as your original."

Duplicate Bishop, who had worked up quite a sweat, grabbed a towel from a nearby chair. "I'm sure you didn't ask me over just to tell me that," he said.

"Of course not," Duplicate Justin replied. "Look around you. What do you see?"

Duplicate Bishop was confused. "Tennis courts?"

"Money! Power!" Duplicate Justin exclaimed. "The Wellingtons belong to lots of clubs just like this one. In four different countries! They have their hands in dozens of companies! Do you know what I could do with all that?"

"But you're not real. You're just a duplicate of the original Justin. When he returns, you'll have to leave."

"What if he doesn't return?"

"Why wouldn't he?"

Duplicate Justin flashed an evil smile. "What if something tragic happened to him and he never came back? I could take his place and nobody would be the wiser."

"My original would know, and so would Miss Mann."

"They could be taken care of, too."

"What are you suggesting?"

"I was just thinking about the possibility of becoming permanent. Don't you wish to become permanent?"

"Oh yeah, of course I would like to be permanent. And while you're at it, why don't you get us a billion dollars?"

Duplicate Justin moved menacingly toward Duplicate Bishop. "I'm serious!"

Duplicate Bishop stood his ground. "What is your problem?"

"Nothing," Duplicate Justin lied. "I've just had a lot on my mind lately. There's a lot involved in being a Wellington, you know."

"Yeah, well, maybe I should be heading home now. There's a lot involved being a Chance, too." Duplicate Bishop looked down at the expensive tennis shirt and shorts he was wearing. "I better go change. Thanks for loaning me these clothes," he said.

"Keep them," Duplicate Justin offered. "I've got four closets full of clothes at the mansion. Hey, do you want me to call a limo to take you home?"

Duplicate Bishop shook his head. "No. That would never happen with my original. I'll take my bike. Gramps would get suspicious if I pulled up in a limo."

"Your grandfather runs a tight ship," Duplicate Justin said. "You're not afraid of him, are you?"

Duplicate Bishop walked to a nearby cabana and grabbed the t-shirt and jeans he had worn to the country club. "He's not that bad once you get used to him. He's just got a lot of rules. He must drive the real Bishop crazy. I'll see you later."

"Count on it," Duplicate Justin said as Duplicate Bishop walked away. Duplicate Justin then retrieved his own clothes from the cabana. As he grabbed his jeans, a small glowing object fell out of one of the pockets. It appeared to be a pen. Duplicate Justin studied it carefully.

"Onyx gave this to my original," he mumbled to himself. "I'll bet he had this thing on him when Miss Mann created us. She must have also created a duplicate of this, too. I wonder if it works." Duplicate Justin clicked the device three times. "Well if it does, I'm calling for you, Onyx. We've got some talking to do."

Duplicate Justin absentmindedly twirled the pen in his hand as he pulled out his cell phone and called for a limo to take him home. He failed to notice that the pen was now flashing.

Duplicate Justin strolled down the front walk of the country club to the driveway where the limo was waiting. The car sped away before he had fully climbed in, throwing him against the seat.

Duplicate Justin struggled to sit upright. "Hey, you idiot!" he screamed at the driver. "What do you think you're doing?"

The driver didn't say a word. He just continued driving at a faster speed, taking sharp turns that tossed Duplicate Justin around the limo.

"Hey! Whoever you are! When we get out of here, you are so fired!" he said as he slammed from side to side. Then just as quickly as it had started, the limo came to a sudden stop, throwing Duplicate Justin to the floor.

As Duplicate Justin climbed back onto the seat, the limo door opened and a tall thin man with a mess of black hair entered. He was dressed all in black. As he sat across from Duplicate Justin the limo took off.

"Who are you?" Duplicate Justin asked. "And get out of my limo."

The man smiled a toothy grin. "You summoned me, Justin."

Duplicate Justin shook his head. "I never summoned you. I don't even know who you are."

"Yes you do," the man replied. "Look closer."

Duplicate Justin studied the man's face. A sudden, horrible memory flashed through his mind. "Wait a minute!" he said. "I do recognize you! You're one of Onyx's emissaries!"

"Yes. I am Silhouette."

"You're the guy who kidnapped everyone and brought them to Onyx's lair, back when all this started. What are you doing here?"

"You summoned me when you activated the tracking device."

Duplicate Justin pulled the tracking device from his pants pocket. "I thought it was supposed to summon Onyx."

Silhouette became very agitated. "Onyx is not at your beck and call. He sent me. There are two questions he wants answered."

"Like what?" Duplicate Justin asked.

"First, why did you summon him?"

"And?"

The man snatched the tracking device from Duplicate Justin's hand. "And why are there two tracking devices?"

Duplicate Justin grabbed the tracking device. "Onyx gave that to me! Actually, he gave it to my original. When Miss Mann created us, she must have unknowingly also made a duplicate tracking device."

Silhouette nodded his head. "That explains a lot. You and your companions are duplicates. Which means that the originals are after the clues. So, Christie Rae has been fooling around creating her duplicates again? I thought she had given up on those. They never turn out right."

"Hey! I resent that!"

Silhouette held up his hand. "Present company excluded. So why have you called for Onyx?"

"I want to know if he can make me permanent. I don't want to disappear when my original comes back."

"Ah, you seek to extend your existence. I'm sure that Onyx can help you. But before he does, you must do something for him first."

"Sure," Duplicate Justin said. "Anything. Just name it."

"Onyx has his doubts about your original. He may need to be taken out of the picture. You might be asked to do the deed if necessary. You don't have any problems with that, do you?"

Duplicate Justin shook his head. "No. But I may need some help in doing it."

"What about your companions?" Silhouette asked. "Would they be up to the task? Do they also seek to become permanent?

"I think so. I bet I can talk them into it."

"You must be sure. They are either with us, or against us. You will be contacted again shortly. Find out who is an ally and we will talk further."

The limo stopped once again. Silhouette stepped out of the car and simply disappeared.

# Chapter 7

## Speed Reader

Bishop, Gary, Mandy and Justin arrived in Key West, Florida, a festive community located at the southernmost point of the United States. After checking into one of the beautiful hotels on the harbor, they went in search of a library to find an answer to their latest clue.

They walked past a pier filled with entertaining street performers and vendors. Since the temperature was in the eighties, most of the sun-tanned onlookers were dressed casually. Out at sea they saw dozens of sailboats. Everywhere they looked, people were enjoying themselves. They each wished that they could also relax and enjoy the surroundings.

Once they located the Key West public library, they wasted no time pouring through dozens of books about ships and shipwrecks. They stacked the books on a large table.

"Who would have thought there were so many shipwrecks?" Mandy mused.

Justin was leafing through a large book when something caught his attention. "Here's a ship that went down one hundred years ago, and it was carrying two hundred pounds of gold! We could stop and look for that one along the way."

"We're not here to look for gold," Bishop replied.

"Now I know why my family is wealthy and your family isn't," Justin sniffed.

At that moment an elderly female librarian walked over to Justin. She was carrying several old musty books.

"Excuse me. I found that book you requested."

"What book?" Justin asked. "I didn't request a book."

The librarian was firm. "I believe you did. It's about doubling your personal wealth in thirty days or less."

This sparked Justin's interest. "Yeah," he said. "You must have read my mind."

"It can't leave the reference section. If you'll follow me I'll take you to it."

"I'll be right back, guys," Justin said. He got up and followed the librarian into a deserted part of the library. He looked around suspiciously. "Where is this reference section? Cuba?"

The librarian dropped her books and turned to face Justin. She was scowling. When she spoke, her voice dropped several octaves.

"Alright, kid. Give me an update on Bishop."

Justin was stunned. "Bishop? What are you talking about? Who are you?"

The librarian's face morphed into a two horned demon with glowing red eyes and the same demented smile Justin had earlier seen on the face of Erik the flight attendant. She grabbed Justin by the shirt with one clawed hand.

"I am your worst nightmare! Tell me what's taking you so long! Onyx sent me here to speed things up."

Justin cringed. "Uh, we're here trying to find the next clue. For our quest! We think it has to do with a shipwreck."

The librarian's face returned to normal. "A shipwreck?" she asked, releasing Justin. Suddenly she burst off at a blinding speed. Justin had a hard time watching her as she ran up and down numerous aisles pulling books off shelves and flipping through their pages at super human speed. Then she stopped as suddenly as she had begun. She opened one particular book and handed it to Justin.

"There! On page 98! That's what you're looking for. If you need anymore help, don't be afraid to ask. That's why I'm here."

The librarian smiled a nasty smile and exited. Justin returned to Bishop, Mandy and Gary, who were still busy pouring through books.

"Hey guys," Justin said as he held up the book. "I've found a listing for a French ship that sank over fifty years ago about forty miles off the coast of Key West. Its name was Le Roi Blanc. You couldn't ask for a better clue." Justin noticed the puzzled looks on his friends' faces. "Don't you get it? Le Roi Blanc is French for The White King. Alabaster was your father's name. Alabaster is also a white stone. So a white king can also be an alabaster king. King Alabaster!"

Mandy was impressed. "I didn't know you knew French," she said.

Justin smiled. "I picked it up on the French Riviera. We go there every year, too. You wouldn't believe what those French babes wear on the beach. Or what they don't wear."

"Since Justin is such an expert on everything, he should rent us a boat," Gary suggested. "Then you can go diving for the next clue."

The librarian peered at Justin from around a corner while Gary was speaking. Her eyes were glowing red again. A nervous Justin suddenly wanted to get out of there. Fast!

"For once, you're right, Jumbo," he said to Gary. "I know boats. My father has several. I'll go find us one." Justin rushed out of the library.

"He's acting real weird," Gary said. "Even more than usual. I wonder what he's up to?"

The four adventurers were on board an old fishing boat within the hour, bound for the open sea. Bishop and Mandy were in their bathing suits, preparing to don their scuba gear. Justin, also in a bathing suit, was talking to the captain. Gary, still fully dressed, sat quietly by himself, sucking on a lollipop. After a few moments, Justin strolled over to Mandy. As he spoke he began putting on his scuba gear.

"You look really terrific in that bathing suit, Mandy."

"Thank you, Justin. I didn't think anybody was going to notice." Mandy glanced at Bishop.

"I noticed. I just didn't get around to mentioning it," Bishop said. "You look great."

"Do you have any idea where we're going?" Mandy asked Justin. "Or how long this is going to take?"

"The captain says he's been to the Le Roi Blanc before, and we should be there soon."

"If people have been there before, how do we know that we'll find what we're looking for?" Mandy asked. "Somebody else may have found it before us, whatever it is."

"I don't think so," Justin said. "Neither the captain nor anyone else who has tried salvaging the wreck has ever stayed around. Too many strange things kept happening to them and their equipment. He thinks we're a little crazy coming out here. In fact, I had to pay him three times his normal fee before he would even consider it."

"Let's just hope we're all alive for the trip back," Gary said as he joined the group. He was still in his clothes.

"Aren't you going to change?" Mandy asked.

"Nah. I think I'll stay on the boat. One of us should stay up here, don't you think?"

"I think you're too fat to fit into a bathing suit," Justin laughed. "Don't worry, blubber butt, the captain must have a crowbar."

"I'll tell you what you can do with your crowbar," Gary growled.

Bishop stepped between them. "Guys! Knock it off, okay?"

"Honestly, Justin, sometimes you can be such a jerk," Mandy said as she turned and walked away. Justin followed her. "I was just kidding, Mandy," he insisted. "Don't get mad."

"I think you should dive with us," Bishop said to Gary. "We should stay together."

"Look, don't tell the others, but I'm afraid of the water. It's killing me just being on this boat. I really can't go down there."

"There's nothing to be afraid of."

"You guys are all swimmers. I'm not. Let's leave it at that," Gary said.

Mandy and Justin rejoined Bishop and Gary. "Justin has something he wants to say," Mandy hinted.

"I'm sorry I called you blubber butt, O'Leary. And I didn't mean what I said about the crowbar. I'm sure we could figure out a way to get your butt in a bathing suit without one."

"Justin!" Mandy sighed.

"C'mon, Mandy! Gimme a break! I'm new at this. I never apologized to anyone before."

"Apology accepted, for now," Gary said.

"Gary is gonna stay on the boat." Bishop sounded authoritative. "He'll keep an eye on things up here."

"Do you two know how to use this equipment?" Justin asked. "We should have enough oxygen for about an hour. If we don't find anything before that time, we'll have to come up and get more oxygen." Justin produced two portable flashlights. "You should also tie these around your wrists."

"I'm ready whenever you are," Mandy said.

"Bish, do you have your dagger?" Gary asked. "In case you need it down there?"

Bishop tightened his belt. "It's right here. Okay, team. Let's go! See you in sixty, Gar."

Gary watched as Bishop, Mandy and Justin fell into the water. He then reached into his pocket and pulled out another lollipop. "Good luck, guys. You too, Justin. I guess."

Bishop, Mandy and Justin were dazzled by schools of multi-colored fish as they slowly descended into the ocean. Shiny red crabs and bright blue lobsters scuttled about below. They stopped for a few seconds and admired the coral formations. Bishop regretted not having brought along a camera. Justin pointed to a barracuda off in the distance. Eventually they dove toward a sunken ship, which Justin recognized as the Le Roi Blanc.

As they swam around the large wreck looking for a way inside, they did not see the mysterious humanoid entity watching them from the murky darkness.

# Chapter 8

## Sink or Swim

Bishop, Mandy and Justin came upon an opening in the side of the Le Roi Blanc. It looked like someone had blown a hole in its hull.

Justin aimed his flashlight through the opening and was dazzled by what he saw inside. Pile after pile of gold coins. "I'm rich!" Justin thought, briefly forgetting that he was already the heir to a vast fortune.

Bishop and Mandy pushed Justin to one side and looked through the opening. They, too, were thrilled with their discovery. Once his initial excitement subsided, Bishop couldn't believe that previous divers hadn't discovered this fortune in gold. Something wasn't right.

As Bishop pondered and Mandy gaped, Justin swam through the hole and into the murky room. Once inside, and to his horror, Justin saw that it was filled with more than gold coins. The rotted remains of previous explorers were scattered everywhere.

He reached out to carefully touch one skeletal figure. Its skull came loose, floating toward Justin's face. He shrieked and pushed away, anxious to rejoin his two friends. But Bishop and Mandy were no longer watching from outside the hole. They were gone. Now totally scared, Justin swam for the opening, only to be ensnared by a net.

Struggling to break free, Justin stirred up sediment from the floor of the room, further obscuring his vision. The more Justin fought against the net, the more entangled he became. He could hardly move. He could not see. He was terrified.

Suddenly, something was pulling on the net. A helpless Justin was dragged through the darkness to a room dimly illuminated by two overhead lights. There was so much sediment floating in the water that Justin's visibility was severely compromised. He saw a shadowy figure approaching. He struggled once again to escape the net, certain that this mysterious entity meant to harm him. And then a hand grabbed his arm. This was it! The entity moved closer.

Justin was finally able to see his captor. He seemed to be about twelve years old. He had blue-green hair and was wearing a purple bathing suit. He had no underwater breathing gear.

As the boy swam away, Justin noticed two other figures in the gloom. Bishop and Mandy! What was going on?

Bishop and Mandy swam over to Justin and tried to free him from the netting. Meanwhile, the boy worked some controls on the far wall. Within seconds, the water was quickly pumped out of the room. Bishop, Mandy and Justin still wore their scuba gear. "You can take that equipment off," the boy said. "It is now safe for you to breathe in here." Bishop, Mandy and Justin tentatively began removing their breathing equipment. "I do not think any of you should try anything foolish, like trying to overpower me," the boy warned. "I am a lot stronger than I look. I can take all three of you on with no problem. In fact, I just did. As easily as catching fish. Those fake gold coins work every time."

"You set a trap for us!" Bishop flared.

"You were trespassing," the boy countered. "I merely moved things along. I don't like trespassers."

Mandy lifted her facemask off her head. "What do you want from us?"

"Your people have always come here to take what is not yours. Tell me who you are, and what you are doing here."

Bishop stepped forward. "My name is Bishop, and these are my friends. We're searching for something."

"Searching for what? Gold? Everyone comes down here searching for gold. Is that all you surface dwellers care about? Gold?"

"We're not interested in gold," Bishop said. "We don't know what we're looking for, exactly. Who are you, anyway?"

"My name is Aquarian. I have lived here ever since my parents died. They were murdered by surface dwellers like you! That is why I trust no one from the world above! Now, for the last time, tell me why are you here!"

"All I can tell you is that we are looking for something that my father might have left here," Bishop explained. "We don't know what it is. All we know is that it is a clue to where we have to go next. We're on an expedition."

"What kind of expedition?" Aquarian demanded.

"I can't tell you," Bishop replied. "Here, let me prove to you that you can trust us." Bishop removed his dagger from his belt and offered it to Aquarian.

Justin was incredulous. "Are you crazy? This guy could gut us like fish!"

"Don't tempt me," Aquarian remarked, with no discernable emotion.

"That dagger is our only weapon," Bishop explained. "Now will you trust us?"

Aquarian stared at the dagger. His eyes focused on the strange designs on its handle. "Where did you get this?"

"It belonged to my father. Why?"

"I have seen markings like these before, on something my father gave me before he was killed. He said that I was to guard it with my life until he, or someone he sent, came for it. He said someone very important gave it to him."

"This thing Aquarian is talking about might be the next clue!" Mandy exclaimed.

"My father said that I was to show it only to the person who knew the password," Aquarian said with continued coldness.

Bishop frowned. "I don't remember my father telling me about a password in any of his messages."

"Oh, great!" Justin groaned. "We're stuck on the ocean floor, kept prisoner by a nut-job who has our only weapon, and you don't even know a stupid password. What an organized group. What did I do to deserve this?"

Aquarian was clearly disgusted with Justin. "I think I will slaughter you, first," he remarked.

Justin was silent.

Aquarian turned to Bishop and Mandy. "I cannot stay out of water for too long a period of time. So, if you cannot prove who you are, right now, then I will have to get rid of you. The easiest way would be to fill this room back up with water. Even if you managed to get your breathing devices back on, your air would eventually run out."

"You can't kill us!" Mandy protested. "We've told you that we mean you no harm!"

"This is going nowhere. I think I will flood the room now."

"No!" Mandy screamed.

Stepping to the controls, Aquarian began pushing buttons and setting dials. He did not notice Bishop standing nearby, talking under his breath. Aquarian did, however, notice that there was no response from the controls.

"Something is wrong! I cannot get the controls to work! If I don't get this room flooded again I will be in trouble!"

"That works for me, creep," Justin sneered.

Aquarian was losing his cool. "I cannot get the door open, either! If I don't get into water soon, I'll die!"

Now Bishop had the upper hand. "Maybe if you answer a few of our questions we can help you get out of here. Who built this room, anyway? It couldn't have been part of the ship to begin with. It's way too modern."

"All I know is that it was built by the man whose secret I am here to protect."

"That had to be my father!" Bishop smiled for the first time since they entered the ship. "Now, what about the object he left behind? And forget the password! Tell us now, or we won't help you!"

Aquarian sat on the floor. He was breathing very heavily. "He said that you would know how to find what you sought. The only clue you need to know is that things aren't always what they appear to be."

Justin groaned. "That sounds like the kind of clue your father would give."

"There's only one thing in this room that can't be what it appears to be," Bishop said with sudden certainty.

"What?" Mandy asked.

"Him!" Bishop pointed to Aquarian. "I think that this has all been a test to see if we are who we say we are. Tell me who you really are, kid!"

"I was left here by King Alabaster as a means of giving his next clue to his son Bishop, if he were to ever appear here," Aquarian replied.

"He already told you he was Bishop!" Justin protested. "Why didn't you give him the freakin' clue?"

"I could not be sure if he was the real Bishop or an imposter." Aquarian turned to Bishop. "You were right. This has all been a test so you could prove you were really Alabaster's son."

"So all that stuff you told us about your parents dying and not being able to breathe and everything else was just a bunch of bull?" Justin was indignant. "Why are you telling us everything now? It doesn't make sense."

"It's as if I no longer have any control over my actions," Aquarian said. "Like someone else is controlling me. I don't know what's happening."

"You're an android, aren't you?" Bishop asked. It was more a statement than a question.

"Yes."

Mandy was puzzled. "An android? What's that?"

"It's a robot created to look like a person," Bishop said. "It would explain a lot. First off, if Aquarian meant to harm us he wouldn't have brought us here. He would have just let us drown. So he must have been looking for someone. Second, he answered my questions. Being a machine he would have to do what I asked. Get up, Aquarian. And tell me, what message do you have from my father?"

Aquarian stood very rigid. His eyes were fixed straight ahead. He began to speak, but in the voice of Alabaster.

"Bishop, you have done well to get this far. But there is more trouble ahead. The closer you get to your goal, the more danger awaits you. I know that Aquarian will see to it that only you, and whoever is traveling with you, will ever hear this message. I have hidden a crucial piece of the device that will allow you to travel to the Homeworld. Find the piece and return it to its proper place, and you will be able to open the portal. And remember, it will be the end of both of our worlds if Onyx gains control of it. If you are observant and pay attention to everything and everyone you meet, you will be able to find it. I have programmed Aquarian to join you on your journey. His strength and durability should be useful to you in your travels. The next part of your quest will take you quite far, and yet, not very far at all. To find the missing piece, you must seek out a statue in a place where your heart is always found. Good luck, my son. May you stay free from the darkness and travel all your life in the light."

Silence followed. As always, Bishop was somewhat stunned by the communication from his father. Aquarian was the first to speak. "It appears that I have to travel with you, although I would rather stay here."

Justin was snide. "Well, why don't you?"

"Because, you stupid human, I was created to follow the orders of Alabaster. He has commanded me to follow Bishop, and I must obey."

"Don't worry, Aquarian. Once we're done, you can come back here if you want," Bishop said.

"You said you had seen markings like those on Bishop's knife on another object," Justin recalled. "Or was that part of your big fake story, too?"

"Yeah, I forgot about that," Bishop remarked. "Show us this thing with the markings, Aquarian."

Aquarian reached toward his chest and opened a panel revealing his micro circuitry. Mandy gasped. On the reverse side of the panel were markings identical to those on the knife handle. Once Aquarian closed the panel neither Bishop, Justin or Mandy could see the seam. They were speechless.

Bishop and his friends silently donned their gear. Aquarian filled the room with water and opened the door to the outside. They all swam to the surface, where the boat was waiting for them.

Gary was sitting on the edge of the deck, eating a lollipop and staring out to sea. He smiled when his friends surfaced. Then he eyed Aquarian. "Hey, Bish! Who's the kid with the weird hair?"

"It's a long story, Gary. He'll be traveling with us for a while. His name is Aquarian."

"Did you find any clues down there?"

"Yes, but let's discuss it later in private, where we won't be overheard by anyone." Bishop looked towards the captain. He had learned not to trust strangers.

Bishop and his friends boarded the boat. As they walked toward their clothes, which were lying in a pile by the cabin, Justin saw his pen sticking out of his shirt pocket. The pen was glowing red. Before any of the others could notice, Justin picked up the shirt and pushed the pen deeper into the pocket. He knew that as long as he stayed with Bishop, Onyx would know all he needed to know.

# Chapter 9

## Double Trouble

Things were not running smoothly back home in Connecticut. While Bishop, Gary, Mandy and Justin were ending their adventure down in Florida, their duplicates gathered together in Bishop's living room for an important meeting. Andrew Chance was once again visiting the Wellington senior center, so they had the house to themselves.

Duplicate Justin was holding court. "Onyx's aide told me if we side with him, Onyx will make us permanent once our originals are destroyed! You cannot hold any loyalty to your originals."

"I don't trust Onyx, and you shouldn't, either," Duplicate Bishop said. "Remember what Miss Mann told us."

"Miss Mann is a loser."

Duplicate Mandy scowled. "Justin! That's a terrible thing to say!"

"Yeah, and besides, you didn't even talk to Onyx," Duplicate Gary countered. "You spoke to one of his minions. How do you know he can really make us permanent? I wouldn't believe it unless I heard it from Onyx himself."

Just as his original would do, Duplicate Gary produced a lollipop from his pocket. He studied the treat carefully, looking somewhat perplexed. "Is anyone else having trouble settling into their body?" Duplicate Gary asked.

"No," Duplicate Mandy replied. "Are you?"

"I can't get a handle on this. I keep making mistakes," Duplicate Gary said as he stuck the lollipop in his ear.

Duplicate Mandy winced. "Doesn't that hurt?"

"Doesn't what hurt?" Duplicate Gary asked.

Duplicate Bishop interrupted the lollipop conversation. Of all the duplicates, he was the most concerned about keeping up appearances on behalf of their originals. "C'mon, Mandy, we have to get to a swim meet. We don't want to be late."

"Are you coming with us, Justin?" Duplicate Mandy asked.

Duplicate Justin was smug. "I don't need to go to the meet. I have more important things to do."

Duplicate Gary also had outside concerns. "I have to help out at my parents' store again. That seems to be all that my original does all day. Work, work, work. And eat, eat, eat."

Duplicate Justin was stunned. "You're complaining about eating?"

"No," Duplicate Gary replied. "Just the work, work, work part."

"If you were working with Onyx, you would be able to goof off as much as you wanted," Duplicate Justin noted.

Duplicate Bishop frowned. "Any more talk about Onyx and I'm gonna call Miss Mann," he warned. He then took Duplicate Mandy's hand and left.

Duplicate Justin turned to Duplicate Gary. "Miss Mann, huh? What can she do?"

"One thing's for sure. She can't create good duplicates," Duplicate Gary said as he stuck the lollipop in his nose. "See what I mean?"

Duplicates Bishop and Mandy walked side by side with identical gym bags slung on their backs. Slowly and quietly they headed to Wellington High School, where the swim meets were held. Finally Duplicate Bishop broke the silence. "Mandy, what do you think about all this?"

"What do you mean?"

"I mean, this feels great, doesn't it? Being alive! Being together! I want this to last, don't you?"

Duplicate Mandy smiled. "Of course I do. This has been wonderful."

"I'm afraid to lose what we have, but on the other hand, it wouldn't be right to take it away from the others," Duplicate Bishop continued. "The only way we could become permanent is by going to Onyx and helping him destroy our originals."

Duplicate Mandy put her arm around Duplicate Bishop. "I don't want to lose you, either. But, on the other hand, I don't want this to end badly. I'm worried about the stupid mistakes I've been making."

"We've all been making mistakes. It seems that when Miss Mann created us, she missed a few things." The two duplicates approached the doorway of the school. "We're late. We'd better hurry."

Once inside, they headed for the pool. "See you in the water," Duplicate Mandy said as she walked toward the girls' locker room. Duplicate Bishop watched her for a few moments. He wondered if it was indeed possible for an artificially created being to fall in love.

Suddenly, a brash voice jolted Duplicate Bishop back to reality. It was the swimming coach.

"It's about time you got here, Chance! Where's Wellington? Have you seen him?"

"Um, I think Justin's sick or something. He's not coming."

"Get your suit on! The rest of the team is in the pool waiting for you. And remember, stay focused!" the coach barked.

Duplicate Bishop entered the boys' locker room and dropped his gym bag on the floor in front of his locker. As he started to get undressed he turned to another boy, the only other person in the locker room.

"Hey, Billy."

"Hey, Bishop. How's it going?" Billy grabbed his towel and started for the door to the pool.

"I've got the feeling that something's wrong, but I just can't put my finger on it," Duplicate Bishop said, but Billy didn t hear him.

One end of the Wellington School poolroom was filled with boys warming up for the meet. The girls' team was at the opposite end. As Bishop entered the poolroom from the boys' locker room his teammates burst into laughter. From across the pool, the girls began laughing, too.

The coach glared at Duplicate Bishop. "What is this? Some kind of stupid joke?"

Duplicate Bishop was suddenly feeling very paranoid. "What do you mean?" he asked.

"Very funny, mister! Or should I say miss?" the coach bellowed, prompting new waves of laughter from the kids in the pool.

Looking down at himself, Duplicate Bishop realized that he was wearing Duplicate Mandy's bathing suit! He had taken her gym bag by mistake. He hadn't even realized that he had put on the wrong bathing suit! This explained his earlier fear that something was wrong.

Duplicate Bishop blushed, all the way down his chest. "Uh, sorry, coach," he squeaked. "I'll go change."

"Forget it, Chance. You can sit this one out. In fact, you can sit the rest of the season out! This is the last straw! You're off the team!"

Duplicate Bishop was suddenly taken back, but not by the coach's decision or his teammate's continuing laughter.

"Oh no!" he cried out. "I hope Mandy hasn't made the same mistake!"

Duplicate Bishop ran to the exit. As he dashed into the hall, he collided with Duplicate Mandy. They both crashed to the floor.

Duplicate Bishop saw that Duplicate Mandy hadn't changed. She held up his bathing suit.

"I was hoping to catch you before...before..." Duplicate Mandy began to laugh.

"This isn't funny," Duplicate Bishop sighed.

"I know. I'm sorry." Duplicate Mandy continued to giggle. She couldn't help herself.

"This is my biggest mistake yet," Duplicate Bishop said as he stood up. "I got my original kicked off the team."

While Duplicate Bishop was dealing with the consequences of his mistake at the pool, Duplicate Gary was having a similarly rough time at the O'Leary Confectionery store. He was working behind the counter with his brother Jerry while his parents were busy in the stockroom out back.

Jerry smiled as his friend Jade and her brother Kenny entered the store. This time Jade was wearing a basketball shirt and carrying a basketball.

Jerry greeted his friends. "Hey guys, what's up?"

"We decided to come in for some ice cream before my big game today," Jade replied.

Kenny was sour. "Big game! Big deal!" Kenny always grumbled the same grumble about Jade's athletic pursuits.

"It's not my fault you're too small to make the team," Jade teased.

"Hey, the other day you said he was too small to make the baseball team, too," Jerry recalled.

"Yeah, he's too small to make any team. Mom says that he takes after Dad's side of the family."

"Do not," Kenny wailed.

"Do too! The only team that you made it on was the team at the ballet school," Jade giggled.

Jerry also laughed. "Ballet? You never told me. Where's your tutu?"

"Very funny," Kenny grumbled.

"How about some ice cream?" Jade said.

Duplicate Gary pushed Jerry aside. "Watch out squirt. I'll take her order. What will you have?"

"Do you have any new flavors?" Jade asked.

"Yeah. Vanilla IBM."

"Vanilla IBM? What's that?"

"Vanilla ice cream with duplicate bananas and marshmallows," Duplicate Gary replied.

Jade looked confused. "What are duplicate bananas?"

Duplicate Gary had made another error. "Imitation banana!" he cried. "I meant imitation, not duplicate!"

"Okay, give me two scoops of that," Jade ordered.

Duplicate Gary scooped two scoops of ice cream out of the container and plopped them directly on the counter in front of Jade. Kenny and Jerry stared, wide-eyed, at the mess Duplicate Gary had made.

"Hey! Where's the cone?" Jade asked, looking at Duplicate Gary as if he were crazy.

"Oh." Duplicate Gary casually grabbed a cone and stuck it point end down into the ice cream. "Sorry about that. Anything else?"

Jerry was concerned. "Are you feeling okay, Gary?"

"Yeah, squirt, don't worry about me," Duplicate Gary said. He turned back to Jade. "Anything else?"

Jerry was still worried about his brother. "Are you really sure you're okay?"

"Yeah, I'm fine." Duplicate Gary was clearly irritated. "If you say one more word, I'm going to cream you."

"But…" Jerry started to say.

"That's it! That's the one word!" Before anyone could move, Duplicate Gary pulled out a canister of whipped cream and sprayed it at his brother's face. Then Duplicate Gary grabbed a fist-ful of cherries and plopped them on Jerry's head.

"Hey look," Kenny laughed. "Gary made a new flavor. Cherry on Jerry!"

Jade was stunned. Jerry didn't move. He simply stood still, looking like a hastily concocted sundae.

Duplicate Gary heard the unmistakable sound of his father's throat being cleared. He turned around and saw his parents standing in the back of the store. They weren't happy. Barry O'Leary looked at Duplicate Gary and pointed to the front door. "Go home, Gary. Immediately. We'll deal with you later."

Without saying a word, Duplicate Gary grabbed a nearby milk shake and scurried outside. Mary O'Leary hurried over to Jerry and began wiping his face with a washcloth. This was more embarrassing to Jerry than the attack by his brother. Jade and Kenny silently sat at the counter as Barry prepared a snack for the both of them.

Meanwhile, Duplicate Gary stopped at a bench down the street from his parents' store. He looked upset, as if he had suddenly realized how serious his mistakes had become. He tried to drink some of the milk shake, but he had trouble keeping the straw out of his nose.

"Ow! Stupid straw!"

Duplicate Gary threw the straw onto the ground and tried to drink the milk shake, but poured half of it down the front of his shirt—just as Duplicate Justin and a stranger approached from down the street. The stranger was wearing a dark gray business suit. His face was hidden behind sunglasses and a wide-brimmed hat.

Duplicate Justin greeted his friend. "Hey, Gary. What're you doing out here? I thought you had to work."

"I've made so many mistakes that my own family threw me out!" Duplicate Gary sighed. "I don't care. It's just stupid work anyhow."

"I brought this guy to meet you. He's one of Onyx's men. I told him what you said about wanting to meet Onyx and he said that he could arrange it."

"Shouldn't we ask the others before we start making any deals?" Duplicate Gary asked.

"Forget them," Duplicate Justin replied. "I want my freedom, and I can't get it until the original Justin is out of the way. I've come up with a plan. We go to where our two originals are and kill them, taking their place without the original Bishop or Mandy finding out. Then we can arrange for Bishop and Mandy to fall into a trap. They'll be right where Onyx wants them. As a reward he'll give us anything we want, just as he promised my original. We can be here permanently and we won't make all these stupid mistakes."

Duplicate Gary looked at Duplicate Justin's feet. He was wearing one dress shoe and one sneaker.

"Wait a minute," Duplicate Gary said. "You said Onyx promised your original anything he wanted?"

Duplicate Justin nodded. "Yeah, he's working with Onyx by keeping him aware of their location. But he doesn't have the guts to do anything more. I can, and I will."

Duplicate Gary grew doubtful. "It sounds like Onyx has the upper hand. But how do we know that he can make us permanent?"

The silent stranger came to life. "Onyx can do anything!"

"Oh, yeah? How can you be so sure?" Duplicate Gary replied.

The stranger morphed into Onyx.

"Oh," Duplicate Gary croaked, almost dropping his milk shake.

"I knew that I could count on you two," Onyx said, with more than a trace of malevolence in his voice. "I can use a couple of new emissaries. I recently had to dispose of a few."

"Why?" Duplicate Justin asked.

"They made a foolish error. Or should I say, a fatal error? They were sent to test the extent of Bishop's power. Instead, they almost killed him in a plane crash. I have seen to it that they will not make any more errors. Ever!"

"A lot of people are screwing up these days," Duplicate Gary said.

"Now then, if you are to join up with me, you must first get rid of the Bishop and Mandy duplicates. They are only going to complicate matters."

"How do we do that?" Duplicate Justin asked.

"You simply kill them. It's that easy! Do as I say and I'll reward you with your lives."

"And if we don't?" Duplicate Gary asked.

"I will dispose of you, as well!" Onyx said with deadly directness. He then wrapped his cape around himself and disappeared.

"He drives a hard bargain," Duplicate Gary grumbled.

Duplicate Justin was undeterred. "Let's go. We have two duplicates to kill."

"Just like that?" Duplicate Gary was hesitant. "You're all set to go kill people?"

"You're not going to wuss out on me, are you?"

"Let me think about it while I finish this milk shake." Duplicate Gary brought the shake to his mouth and poured more of it into his lap.

Meanwhile, Duplicate Bishop and Duplicate Mandy had decided to visit Christie Rae Mann and seek her advice. They found her sitting in a chair in her backyard tinkering with a small metallic device.

"Hello!" Miss Mann smiled.

"Hi, Miss Mann," they both replied.

"I've been trying for years to get this device working again. I think the problem is that the parts I need haven't been invented on this world yet." Miss Mann placed the object on a small table. "Ah well, what can I do for you two today? Is anything wrong?"

"Well, it's like this," Duplicate Bishop began. "We're making a lot of mistakes. A lot of very stupid mistakes. Something must be going wrong with us. Is there anything you can do to help?"

Miss Mann offered a sympathetic smile. "I'm afraid I'm out of practice, Bishop. As your time limit approaches, you'll probably find yourselves making more and more mistakes, more frequently. Where are Gary and Justin? Are they having the same problems that you two are having?"

"Yes, but they seem to be acting differently from us. Justin actually said that we should team up with Onyx and try to make ourselves permanent. And I think Gary agrees with him."

Miss Mann frowned. "I see. And how do you two feel about that?"

"We'd like to live. But we both feel that not existing would be better than teaming with somebody as evil as Onyx," Duplicate Bishop replied.

Miss Mann stood up. "I just want to say that I am very proud of you both. You've made the right choice. While it may be possible for

Onyx to prolong your existence, it would be a very bitter existence, I assure you."

Duplicate Mandy was worried about the others. "What are you going to do about Gary and Justin's duplicates?"

"Since there is a good chance that they will join up with Onyx and create more trouble, I have no choice but to un-create them right now. I'm sorry to sound so cold, but the stakes are very high."

"Can you do that?" Duplicate Mandy asked. "They aren't even here!"

"Fortunately I don't need them here in order to un-create them. The question is, would you two like to be un-created now, or remain a bit longer? The choice is yours. I need to warn you, the mistakes you are making will only get worse, the longer you remain."

Duplicate Bishop held Duplicate Mandy's hand. "Can we talk about this alone?"

"Of course. I'll leave you for a few minutes."

As Miss Mann walked away, Duplicate Bishop picked up the device that she left on the table and began fiddling with it. He then leaned forward and kissed Duplicate Mandy.

"What was that for?"

"I've always wanted to do that, Mandy. If we're going to be un-created, I figure I should do it at least once before I go."

"So you've decided that you want to end your existence?"

"Yes," Duplicate Bishop somberly replied. "It's the only choice."

"I agree." This time it was Duplicate Mandy who did the kissing.

Miss Mann called out from across the yard. "Have you two come to a decision?"

"Yes," Duplicate Bishop said, putting his arm around Duplicate Mandy. "We feel that we should go now, before we do something really stupid that could hurt our originals."

"You are both very wise," Miss Mann smiled. "I hope that your originals are making such good choices."

"While you were gone I fixed this for you." Duplicate Bishop held up the device.

Miss Mann was stunned. "How did you do that?"

"Don't forget. I'm a duplicate of Bishop. I have all his powers and skills, so it was simple to fix that device. It won't give you any more problems."

"Are you both ready?" Miss Mann asked. The duplicates nodded. "Okay, then. This won't hurt at all. At the count of three, both of you, and the duplicates of Justin and Gary, will cease to exist. One, two..."

"Wait!" Duplicate Bishop interrupted. He kissed Duplicate Mandy one last time. "See you when I see you."

Duplicate Mandy smiled. "Not if I see you first."

"Three!" Miss Mann said. The two duplicates faded away in front of her. "Good luck to you both, wherever you are."

Elsewhere, little Jerry O'Leary found his brother talking with Duplicate Justin. They were still seated on the same bench where they had encountered Onyx. Jerry noticed the spilled milk shake in Duplicate Gary's lap.

"Ha ha! You had an accident! You had an accident!" Jerry taunted his brother.

"Shut up, you little squirt!" Duplicate Gary growled, tossing the remains of the shake into Jerry's face with a splash.

"Hey! I'm tellin' ma!" Jerry cried.

Blinded by the shake, Jerry tried to clear his face with his hands. Just then, Duplicate Gary and Duplicate Justin began to fade away.

"What the heck? What's happening to us?" Duplicate Gary exclaimed.

"This is Miss Mann's doing! Onyx will fix her!" Duplicate Justin hissed. They both disappeared just as Jerry cleared the shake away from his eyes. He looked around.

"Where'd you go?" Jerry yelled. "Come back, coward! I'm gonna get you!" Jerry then tasted some of the shake on the back of his hand. "Hmm! Pretty good, if I say so myself."

# Chapter 10

## Can't Buy Me Love

Later that night, after dinner at a seafood restaurant, Bishop, Mandy, Gary, and Justin retreated to their hotel suite with a local specialty: a key lime pie.

"This is delicious," Mandy raved. A glob of meringue had attached itself to the tip of her nose.

"It's as good as Mrs. O'Leary's pies," Bishop said between mouth-fuls.

"No way," Gary objected. "My mom's pies are definitely better."

"Then why have you consumed four slices?" Aquarian asked from the corner of the room. He was still wearing his bathing suit.

Gary smiled. "I could have eaten the whole thing if it were as good as my mom's."

Justin was grouchy. "Forget about the pie and your mother. Isn't anyone thinking about the last stupid clue?"

"Someone's a real grouch tonight," Gary said as he swallowed another forkful of pie.

Mandy stopped eating. "Justin's right. We should try to figure it out."

"Bish, why don't you ask C.H.I.P. if he has any ideas about what we should do next?" Gary suggested.

"Excellent idea," Bishop said. He began fiddling with his watch. "C.H.I.P? Are you there? C.H.I.P?"

There was a long silence as everyone waited for a response. And waited. And waited. And waited.

"I don't understand this," Bishop said. "Why isn't it working?"

Mandy looked at Bishop's watch. "That isn't the correct time. Something must be wrong with it. The last time I had something like that happen was when I wore my watch in the pool."

"Oh, no!" Bishop cried. "I forgot to take the watch off when we went underwater! It must not be waterproof! Now I've lost access to C.H.I.P.!"

"Way to go, wonder boy," Justin groaned.

Mandy shot a disgusted look at Justin. "Don't get all over Bishop for this."

"Yeah," Gary added, shaking a forkful of pie in Justin's direction. "We all make mistakes. Especially you!"

Justin smiled. "If I'm so lame, how come I just figured out the new clue?"

"You did?" Bishop said. "Tell us!"

"I think I know what your father was talking about. He mentioned a place where your heart is always found. There's an old song about someone leaving his or her heart in San Francisco. That must be what he was referring to. We should go there!"

"Oh, I don't know," Mandy sighed. "San Francisco is so far away! We had better be sure."

"Believe me, I'm sure," Justin was decidedly self-impressed.

"You think you're so smart, don't you?" Gary sneered. "You think with all of your money we'll do whatever you want! This is Bishop's quest and he will decide where we go. Don't think you can boss us around just because your parents are rich."

"It's not my fault that the rest of you can't figure out these clues."

"At least we don't wimp out when the going gets tough," Gary said. "You threw up on the plane. You passed out in the airport."

"And you wouldn't go scuba diving!" Justin countered.

"You're useless and you know it," Gary continued. "Why don't you get lost? We don't need you hanging around! Nobody wants you here, anyway! Go back home to your rich mommy and daddy and leave us alone!"

"Fine! I've taken enough from you! All of you! I'm outta here!" Justin barked as he stormed into the next room.

Mandy ran after him. "Justin! Wait!"

Bishop stared at Gary for a few moments. "What was that all about? Why did you turn on him like that?"

"I'm sick of his superior attitude!"

"And maybe a little jealous?" Aquarian asked.

Gary was defensive. "Just because he's rich and good looking and thin doesn't mean I'm jealous!"

Aquarian was smug. "Not much," he said.

"Go soak your head, fish face!" Gary snarled.

Meanwhile, Bishop went to Justin's room, where he found him staring out the window. Mandy was standing beside him.

Justin was quiet. "Leave me alone."

"You can't leave," Bishop said. "We need you."

"No you don't. Nobody needs me!"

"That isn't true," Mandy countered.

"Everywhere I go it's always the same thing! Everybody thinks that just because I'm rich, I have everything."

Mandy spoke softly. "But...you do have everything."

Justin's eyes suddenly filled with tears. "You don't know what it's like when your parents don't speak to one another! They didn't get married because they loved each other. They did it to make a business merger! They wouldn't care if I fell off the face of the Earth. They wouldn't even notice!"

"You can't believe that," Mandy said.

"It's true!" Justin was now crying. "Why do you think I came on this quest, anyway? Just to get away from them!"

"But what about all those trips you told us about?" Bishop asked. "Your family was together on those vacations."

"I travel with our servants! They're the closest friends I have, and that's only because they're paid to be with me! They don't like me, either!" Justin wiped tears off his cheeks with the backs of his hands. "The only friend I have at school is Mandy. The only time anyone else talks to me is if they want something, cause they know I can get it for them. The swim team only likes me because I win all the time!" Justin grabbed his suitcase, which he hadn't unpacked. "This is over! I'm out of here!"

Bishop stepped forward, blocking Justin's exit. "I'll always be your friend," he said. "No matter what happens."

Justin was momentarily stunned by this expression of genuine friendship. It was so foreign to him that he didn't know how to respond, so he simply stepped around Bishop and walked out the door.

Bishop and Mandy watched as Justin moved past Gary in the main room.

"Hey, don't leave on my account," Gary said.

For once, Justin didn't insult Gary. Instead he left without saying a word.

Gary turned and saw Bishop and Mandy staring at him from the doorway of what had been Justin's room. "What are you lookin' at me for?" Gary asked. His friends didn't answer. Gary hastily unwrapped a fresh lollipop.

The following morning, Bishop and Mandy were picking at a room service breakfast. They both looked tired. Gary was eating heartily. Aquarian was silently sitting in the background. Finally, Gary broke the silence.

"You can't blame this Justin thing on me!" Gary said. "This trip hasn't been easy on any of us."

"Nobody is blaming you," Bishop quietly replied.

"Of course you are," Aquarian said to Bishop.

"Did I ask for your opinion?" Bishop growled.

"Admit it. We've all been tough on Justin," Mandy said.

"It's not like he didn't ask for it," Gary replied between heaping forkfuls of scrambled eggs.

"I feel sorry for him," Mandy sighed. "He's so alone! I had no idea."

Bishop picked at a bagel. "This has been rough on all of us. And it all happened so fast. I don't think any of us has had time to let it sink in. Think about what we're doing!"

"You're right," Mandy agreed. "It's kind of overwhelming."

"I'd say we were all dreaming, if these pancakes didn't taste so great," Gary mumbled. His mouth was full.

"I just want life to go back to the way it was before my birthday," Bishop said. "I don't think my heart is in this. I want to go home."

"Wait a minute! That's it! That's the answer to the clue!" Mandy exclaimed. "Your father mentioned going where your heart can be found! He must have meant home!"

Bishop thought for a moment. "If that's the case, then I'll bet he was telling us that the statue we need to find is back home in Wellington! Right in our own backyard!"

Gary frowned. "So he sent us on a big ol' wild goose chase? For nothing?"

"No, not at all," Bishop replied. "I'll bet he wanted us to link up with Aquarian."

"Affirmative!" Aquarian replied.

"We should get home right away," Bishop said. "Our duplicates must be running out of time."

"What about Justin?" Mandy was pensive. "We can't just leave him here in Florida."

"Why not? He's rich. He probably already flew back to Wellington," Gary surmised.

"He didn't sound like he had a home to go home to," Mandy said.

Bishop took charge. "We have to assume he's all right and can find his way back. We need to get to the airport."

Aquarian walked over to Bishop. "I will accompany you to your home," he said.

"Okay, but you should put some clothes on. You can't travel around in a bathing suit." Bishop handed Aquarian a T-shirt and jeans.

Aquarian grimaced. "Ugh. Surface fashion."

"Let's get to the airport," Bishop said. "We are going home! Next stop, Wellington!"

# Chapter 11

## A Random Event

Later that day, Bishop, Mandy, Gary and Aquarian stepped off a small commercial airliner at Wellington Airport. They hailed a taxi and instructed the driver to take them to the town park. All four sat in the crowded back seat. Bishop took a moment to check his ring. It was white. The driver was not one of Onyx's operatives.

"Can't we stop home before we continue searching?" Gary asked. "I'm tired and I'm hungry!"

"You are always hungry," Aquarian observed.

"I am not."

"Shouldn't we check on our duplicates before we go to the park?" Mandy asked.

"I'm sure Miss Mann is keeping tabs on them," Bishop said. "Right now we have to find the next clue. My father said to look for a statue near home. The only statue that I know of in Wellington is in the park."

"You mean the Wellington Computer statue?" Gary asked.

"Yeah," Bishop replied. "I hope that's it."

Once the cab driver deposited them in the park, Bishop and his friends walked directly to the statue. It was a sculpture of a man sitting at a desk with a computer. A sign nearby read, "Wellington, Home of the Wellington Computer."

"Don't tell Justin, but I always thought this statue was kind of tacky," Mandy said.

Suddenly, they all heard a familiar voice from above. "It doesn't look that bad from up here!"

The four looked upward to see a figure descending from the sky.

"Reprint!" Mandy exclaimed.

Still looking like Peter Pan, Reprint hovered over the statue.

"What brings you here?" Bishop asked.

"I was just passing by," Reprint-Pan said as he landed. "Christie Rae Mann contacted me and told me that there was a little trouble with your duplicates. It became necessary for her to un-create them."

Bishop was stunned. "I had better call her."

"No need," Reprint-Pan said. "She has everything under control. So, have you found your next clue yet?"

"No," Bishop said. "It has something to do with this statue, I think."

Reprint-Pan pointed at Aquarian. "Who's he?"

"That's Aquarian. We ran into him in Florida. He's an android built by my father. I got my last clue from him."

Reprint-Pan was taken aback. "An android? How odd." He walked up to Aquarian and looked him over from top to bottom. "He's a wonderful piece of work. I had heard that your father was a genius at machinery. I would never know that this kid wasn't real." As Reprint-Pan spoke he poked a finger into Aquarian's chest.

"Poke me again and I will break your finger off," Aquarian stated.

"Touchy little fellow, isn't he?" Reprint-Pan laughed. "Bet he's a lot of fun to have around. You say that he gave you your last clue. Are you sure that you heard all of it?"

"I think so. I could try again and see if he knows anything else. Aquarian, is there anything more that you can tell me about where we can find our next clue?"

Once again, Aquarian's eyes glazed over and he spoke in Alabaster's voice.

"Son, it is time for you to find the key that you seek. If you are at your final destination, and you are ready, I will instruct you as to where you may locate it."

"We're here, father," Bishop said, as if Alabaster were alive. "Tell me what to do."

"Go to the keyboard and type in your name. What you seek will appear. You will know what to do when you see it. Good luck."

"Are you sure that was your father speaking, Bish?" Gary asked. "He didn't give us a vague clue that time."

Bishop ignored him and looked up at the statue. "There's the keyboard, but it's way out of reach. I guess I'm gonna have to climb up there."

"Let me fly you up," Reprint-Pan offered. He then grabbed Bishop and lifted him to the top of the statue. Bishop looked at the stone keyboard and slowly typed his name on the keys. At first it appeared to have no effect, until the screen on the monitor lowered to reveal a small opening. Bishop could see a small object inside.

"What's in there, Bish?" Gary asked.

"I'm not sure." He reached into the opening and grabbed the object. "It's a chess piece!"

"A chess piece?" Gary exclaimed. "We traveled up and down the East Coast just to find a stupid chess piece?"

Reprint-Pan lowered Bishop to the ground. "Yeah, I guess so. It looks like a piece from our chess set back home. You know, my grandfather told me we've been missing a piece since I was born."

"What piece is it?" Mandy asked.

Bishop smiled. "The bishop! Let's bring it back home and see if it really is the missing piece."

A female voice purred from behind them. "An excellent idea!"

Bishop turned to see a tall, shapely brunette emerging from the nearby bushes. She was dressed in a black outfit similar to Onyx's, but with a lot less material.

"Your company is requested. I don't think I need say who sent me."

Bishop was angered by this latest intrusion. "Who are you?"

"The name is Random, honey. My assignment is to bring you to Onyx one way or another. You really don't want me to get angry. I can get very mean when I'm angry. So why don't you kids just come along with me and nobody will get...."

Before Random could finish what she was saying, Reprint-Pan flew a few feet into the air. "No! You cannot take them," he screamed. "You'll have to get past me!"

"Oh, bother," Random sniffed as she grabbed Reprint-Pan's leg and pulled him down to the ground. She gave him a quick kiss on the cheek and he changed into stone.

"Reprint!" Mandy gasped.

"What did you do to him?" Bishop demanded.

"Did I forget to mention my special talent? I can change any living thing into a statue, and back, if I so desire. Your flighty associate will cause me less trouble this way. Now, will you come along nicely or do I need to make this messy?"

Bishop was panicking. They couldn't be stopped now. Not after all they had been through. Bishop's friends turned to him, unsure of what to do next. Before they could ask, he once again took charge. He looked thoughtfully at his friends. "I think the best thing for all of us to do…is run!"

Bishop, Gary, Mandy and Aquarian instantly ran in different directions. Being the slowest, Gary was almost immediately caught by Random. Before he knew what was happening, Random kissed him and changed him into a statue.

"One down," Random chuckled as she took off after Mandy. Moments later she, too, had been turned to stone.

Bishop started shaking. "Oh, no! No! No!" he cried out. For a moment he thought he might cry. Things were not turning out as planned. Were his friends dead?

"Why don't you just make this easy on both of us?" Random teased. "Your uncle means you no harm. He just wants to talk to you." Random moved briskly toward Bishop, who was momentarily frozen with fear. Before Random could touch him, however, Aquarian tackled her to the ground.

"Leave Bishop alone!" the android ordered. "He is in my care!"

Random was furious. "Well then, little boy, let's see how well you protect him when you become stone!" Random grabbed Aquarian by the arm and gave him a kiss. Nothing happened. Aquarian smiled broadly.

"Your power only works on beings that are alive," Aquarian said. "I don't suffer from that particular ailment."

Aquarian then slammed Random against a tree. "I warn people only once!" he exclaimed.

Suddenly, Aquarian felt his feet leave the ground. Someone was lifting him into the air.

"I told you that you were going to need help with this one, Random!" Aquarian's abductor said. Bishop recognized him instantly as Print, morphed into the guise of Mercury, in Greek mythology the messenger of the gods. Print-Mercury had small wings on his ankles and wore magic sandals, which enabled him to fly. He wore material around his waist that reminded Bishop of a skirt and a metal helmet on his head.

"I told you I could take care of this myself, Print!" Random screamed at the figure above her.

"What's the matter, Random?" Print-Mercury sneered. "Afraid to share the credit when we report to Onyx? This is only fair. You were supposed to leave my brother to me. So we're even!"

Bishop watched helplessly as Print-Mercury flew higher into the sky with a struggling Aquarian until they were out of sight. Then, a small figure came into view, falling at a very high rate of speed. It was an earthbound Aquarian. His body hit the ground with a terrible crash and shattered into many pieces. Electronic parts flew in all directions. Aquarian's head rolled to Bishop's feet, repeating the words, "No harm to Bishop. No harm to Bishop. No harm to Bishop," over and over again.

Bishop was enraged. He had had enough. He pulled out his dagger and charged at Random. "You'll pay for this, you witch!" he cried. Random tried to step out of Bishop's way, but he was too fast. He plunged the dagger into her shoulder. Random screamed and fell to the ground. Bishop was momentarily stunned by what he had done.

Blood poured from the wound in Random's shoulder. "Please...please help me...so much pain...it hurts," she whimpered.

Bishop knelt down for a closer look. This proved to be a mistake in judgment. Random sprang up and kissed him. Bishop changed into a statue.

"The damsel in distress trick works every time," Random smiled. A few feet away, Print-Mercury landed and morphed back to his normal form.

"That Bishop is tougher than he looks," Print said. "Another few inches and that dagger would have done you in. Believe me, that is one powerful blade." Print held up his hand, revealing partially re-grown fingers.

"As long as you are here you can help me load these four statues on the truck," Random said. "And bring that thing, too," she added, pointing to Aquarian's detached head. "It may be of some use to Onyx."

With that, Random and Print lifted the statue Bishop had become. "I sure would hate to be this kid once Onyx gets done with him!" Random said.

# Chapter 12

## What's a Nice Kid Like You Doing in a Place Like This?

Bishop slowly opened his eyes as if awakening from a deep sleep. He looked around and realized that he was lying on his own bed back in his bedroom. Dazed and confused, he sat up and tried to remember what had happened. Had it all been a dream? Not likely...he was still wearing the uniform Miss Mann had given him. He walked around his room, pausing in front of his dresser to gaze at a framed photo of his father and mother. Bishop glanced at the other objects on his dresser: A stack of comic books, a few CDs, an open box of cookies, a photo of his grandfather, a photo of Bishop with the swim team, and his favorite photo, Mandy and him at a carnival.

Bishop then walked to the window and opened it. A gentle breeze blew into the room as he looked out at his same old backyard. He was completely lost in thought as he stared at the early morning sky. From within, he could hear his father's voice: "Don't look to the sky to find your true place, my son. Look inward."

Without thinking he placed his hand in his uniform pocket and produced the chess piece he found in the statue. Then it hit him. How did he get back here? Where were Gary and Mandy? He raced out of his room and down the stairs. His grandfather was reading in the living room.

"Good morning, Bishop," Andrew Chance said. "What in the world are you wearing?"

"Grandpa!" Bishop had never been so happy to see anyone in his life. He ran into his grandfather's arms. He was trembling.

Andrew was taken aback. He had never seen Bishop this upset before. "What's wrong? Tell me."

Bishop tried to fight his tears. "I can't! I've got to go, Grandpa. Right now! It's important!"

Andrew wasn't ready to let Bishop go just yet. "You sit down and talk to me, young man." Bishop was momentarily taken aback by the sudden sternness in his grandfather's voice. "What's that in your hand, Bishop?" Andrew asked.

"This? Uh…just a chess piece."

"Let me have a look," his grandfather ordered.

"I found it earlier. I was going to check and see if it matches the rest of our set."

Bishop handed his grandfather the chess piece. He didn't notice that the stone in his ring was pure black. Andrew walked to the far end of the living room, where a dusty chess set sat atop a small coffee table.

"You know, this chess set belonged to your father. It's always been missing the bishop. I've never gotten around to replacing it." Andrew placed the piece on the chessboard. "Looks like a perfect match to me."

The chess set began to glow. Suddenly, a strange voice filled the room. "The players are all in place!" the voice boomed. "Let the game begin! Initiating holographic program Alpha One."

A three-dimensional image formed beside Bishop. It was Alabaster.

Andrew was dumbfounded. "What is this?" he asked. "What's going on?" Bishop didn't know how to answer his uncle's question.

"Congratulations, my son," Alabaster began. "You have succeeded in your quest and taken the first step to fulfilling your destiny.
By adding the final component, you have activated Checkmate,
my greatest achievement. Checkmate is the most powerful computer that has ever existed on either of our worlds. Among its many
programs is the ability to create a portal to our Homeworld. Activate
this program and assume your rightful heritage. I'm only sorry that
your mother and I cannot be with you at this momentous occasion.
Remember us in your thoughts and be a benevolent ruler. We love
you."

The image of Alabaster faded away. Andrew simply stared at the
space where the hologram had been.

"I can explain this, Grandpa," Bishop began.

Andrew ignored him. "To think that it has been under my nose all
this time," he said, his voice even lower than usual.

"What has?"

"Your father's master computer, boy. I knew that it had to exist somewhere. At first I thought it was C.H.I.P. But C.H.I.P. wasn't powerful enough. It was more powerful than anything this world had to offer, but not even remotely close to what I knew your father could devise."

Bishop had a sudden, awful realization. He looked his grandfather straight in the eye. "Who are you?" he said angrily. "What have you done with my grandfather?"

"Only what I do to anyone who gets in my way, boy. I eliminated him. But that's old business now. It's been so long I've forgotten how I did it."

"What do you mean?" Bishop was frightened. "I saw him a couple of days ago!"

With that, the man in front of him slowly began to change shape. Bishop watched in horror as his "grandfather" morphed into Onyx.

"I killed him shortly after your parents' premature death," Onyx said with a chilling directness.

"You killed my grandfather?"

"Yes." Onyx was detached. "Don't worry. He didn't suffer. What kind of a monster do you think I am?"

Bishop was reeling. "You killed my parents, too. Didn't you? I'll bet that car crash was no accident! You caused it!"

Onyx moved toward Bishop. "Your parents' death was an accident. I had nothing to do with it. Under other circumstances I would have rejoiced over the death of my dear brother, but the timing of his demise was not right. His death delayed my plans to return home."

"Miss Mann was right," Bishop seethed. "You are a monster."

Onyx continued with his story. "I feared I would be trapped here forever. Then I realized that your father would have left you information about your identity, including the means for you to return to our Homeworld. All I had to do was to wait for you to grow up. It was no problem to dispose of your grandfather. With my ability to change shapes, I took his place so I could keep my eye on you. Believe me it was not easy. I never thought I would have to wait thirteen years! What a boring town this is."

Onyx towered over a speechless Bishop. He could see that his nephew was shaking.

"All the offspring of people from our world who are born on this world have their powers at birth. It could be that the onset of your power was delayed because your father was the only one to marry an Earth woman. That could account for the delay. For the longest time I thought you would never get anywhere. The only fun that I had came from walking past your father's foolish operatives without one of them guessing that I was within reach all this time. Think of it, boy. They've spent the last thirteen years protecting you from me, never realizing I've been living in the same house with you! Come! Let me show you something that has been right under your nose all this time."

Onyx pressed a small mark on the wall under the staircase. An opening appeared and he walked through. Bishop slowly followed. They walked down a stone stairwell and entered a familiar room filled with grotesque statues and fiery torches. Bishop's stomach sank. He was back in Onyx's lair.

"You mean to tell me your lair is right under our house?" Bishop gasped.

"Please. Lair sounds so…common. This is my command center."

"Whatever," Bishop replied.

Onyx sat upon his throne. "You might recognize some of my statues over there," he said, gesturing across the room.

Bishop looked to his left. There were the statues that used to be Mandy, Gary and Reprint.

"They make interesting decorations, don't you think? No matter. I am a generous man. I am willing to change them back. But I would like some help from you in return. I am sure that your father has some safety program in his master computer that I may not be able to override. I need you to help me open the portal."

"Set my friends free first," Bishop demanded.

"I hardly think that you are in any position to bargain, nephew."

"I want my friends changed back or you will never get into the computer! Never!"

"Very well," Onyx growled. "To set your little mind at ease, I shall free your friends. Random! Come here! Now!"

Random appeared from the shadows of a far corner. Her shoulder was bandaged.

"Yes, sugar?" she purred.

"I want you to change Bishop's friends back to normal."

"Such a pity. They look much better this way." Random smiled at Bishop as she spoke. She then kissed each of the statues. They slowly came to life as if nothing had happened.

Gary was the first to speak. "Bish, where are we?"

"What happened?" Mandy asked.

"Later, guys. I have a few family issues to deal with."

Reprint turned and saw Print watching him from the shadows.

Onyx flashed his sinister smile yet again. "Now, my boy, I've kept my part of the bargain. It is time for you to keep yours. After all, your grandfather taught you to honor your promises! Ha, ha, ha!"

"Fine! Let's go upstairs and get this over with," Bishop said as he turned and walked towards the stairwell.

Onyx pushed his way ahead of Bishop. "I follow no one. Random, watch these young ones and see that they don't try to escape."

Random smiled at Gary, Mandy and Reprint. "I think it is only fair to warn you all that if you get changed back into statues a second time, there is no coming back to the living again!" she cooed.

Onyx and Bishop slowly walked up the stairs leading to Bishop's living room. The others followed a respectful distance behind.

Onyx and Bishop entered the living room. Bishop walked to the chess set.

"I wish my dear departed brother could be here to witness my victory," Onyx beamed. "At last, Alabaster. I have beaten you!"

Suddenly, Onyx was struck from behind with a resounding thud. He collapsed unconscious to the floor. Seconds later, Mandy, Gary and Reprint entered the living room, followed by Random, who discovered Onyx on the floor.

Random screamed at Bishop. "What have you done? Onyx warned you what would happen if you tried anything! It's back to the statuary for your friends!" She turned toward Gary, who immediately jumped back. "You first, fat boy!"

Before Random could reach for Gary she was also struck from behind. She collapsed unconscious to the floor. Justin stood before his friends with weapon in hand: Bishop's only swimming trophy.

Mandy rushed into his arms. "Justin!" she cried.

"For once I can honestly say that I'm glad to see you, prep!" Gary gushed, squeezing both Justin and Mandy in a great big bear hug.

"What are you doing here?" Bishop asked.

"I came by to see if you were back home," Justin replied. "I needed to tell you guys something. I heard you in the basement...or lair...or whatever it is. Onyx is getting sloppy. He left the door open. So, what's going on here, Chance?"

"I'll tell you as soon as we deal with these two," Bishop replied, looking at Onyx and Random. "It's good to have you back, man."

Bishop ran to a closet in the kitchen and found a long piece of rope. He filled Justin in on everything that had transpired in Wellington as the group tied up the still unconscious Onyx and Random, making sure to triple knot their hands and feet.

"There! That should do it," Bishop said, securing the last knot.

"So, Onyx was disguised as your grandfather all these years, hoping to get his hands on your father's master computer?" Justin asked.

"That's it in a nutshell."

Justin looked worried. "What are you going to do now?"

Before Bishop could answer, Mandy cried out from across the room. She was standing by a bookcase in the far corner, pointing to Aquarian's disembodied head. "Random must have brought that with her when she delivered the rest of us here," Bishop said.

Mandy was trembling. Bishop picked up Aquarian's head. "Aquarian! Are you in there?" There was no response, but Bishop was undeterred. "Tell us what's going on here!" he commanded.

Aquarian didn't answer, but the chess set responded to Bishop's order. It glowed once again, and as the glow intensified, the white king started to morph and slowly changed into a miniature person. Still dressed in royal garb, he rubbed his eyes and in a voice louder than one would have expected, he boomed, "The players are in place! The game has begun!"

"This is way weird," Gary whispered. Mandy and Justin watched in silent awe.

"I am now fully functional!" the miniature king continued. "Please state the nature of the request."

"Who, or rather what, are you?" Bishop asked. He couldn't quite get a handle on the idea of chatting with a five-inch-tall person.

"I am a multi-functional computer created by Alabaster. I am known as Checkmate."

"Are you more powerful than C.H.I.P.?"

"I am far superior to C.H.I.P., Master Bishop. I was made to answer all questions and to open portals, including the portal that will take you back to your father's Homeworld."

Bishop moved closer. "How does the portal work?"

"At your request, and your request alone, I can open a portal for one minute in any location. But I can only create one portal within a twenty-four hour period."

"What do you think, Bishop?" Mandy asked. "Should we give it a try?"

Bishop frowned. "I don't know. Maybe I should call Miss Mann."

"Come on, Bish!" Gary said. "This is it! A chance to go to your father's Homeworld! It's the reason we started this quest in the first place. You can always tell Checkmate here to reopen the portal tomorrow, so that we can come back. Aren't you curious about what we're going to find there after all we've been through?"

Gary's encouragement worked. "You're right," Bishop said. "We've got to do this. Now! We're going to my father's Homeworld!"

Justin spoke next. "I'll stay here and keep an eye on Onyx. Miss Mann will know what to do with him."

"Okay, but be careful," Bishop said. "Be sure to call her right away!" He then turned to Checkmate. "Checkmate, open up a portal, right here, right now!"

The miniature king walked to the middle of the board. After a few seconds the square that he stood on began to rise. Soon he was floating several inches above the board. He gestured toward the middle of the room and a small, neon circle of light appeared. Bishop and his friends had to look away as it grew bigger and brighter. When it stopped growing, it was roughly the size of an oval doorway and its brightness began to dim. The miniature king's tile lowered back into the chessboard.

"Awesome!" Gary exclaimed. "It looks like a giant hole in mid air. Do we just walk through it?"

A loud voice from behind them shook the entire room. "Not quite, my fat little adversary!" Onyx had awakened and freed himself as the portal was being formed. He was holding the ropes in his hands.

"A bit of friendly advice, children," Onyx hissed. "Never tie up a sleeping shape shifter. Once he regains consciousness, he simply changes shape and escapes."

Several of Onyx's emissaries appeared from the doorway under the stairs. Print and Silhouette were among them. Print immediately began untying Random, who was also waking up. Bishop and the others stood between the portal and Onyx.

"Stand aside, nephew," Onyx commanded. "We're going through!" Onyx turned to his followers. "Come! Follow me to the Homeworld! Victory is mine!"

Onyx shoved Bishop to one side and stepped up to the portal. "Random, before we go, take care of that bothersome traitor over there." He pointed to Justin, who tried to move away, but stepped right into Print's clutches.

"Too bad, sugar," Random purred. "If you had stayed with us, I wouldn't be doing this right now." Justin struggled to free himself from Print's grasp, but his captor held firm. Random kissed Justin on the cheek and turned him into stone.

"No!" Mandy shrieked.

Bishop charged at Onyx. "I won't let this happen!"

Onyx grabbed his nephew and brutally threw him across the room into a bookcase. It crashed to the floor, pinning Bishop underneath. Taking full advantage of the distraction, Silhouette, with blinding speed, punched Reprint and shoved Gary into the wall, stunning them both. Onyx then reached out and grabbed Mandy.

"This will ensure your future cooperation, should you choose to follow me to the Homeworld," Onyx said to Bishop. "Goodbye, nephew!"

"Bishop!" Mandy screamed as she, Onyx, Random, Print and Silhouette disappeared into the portal, followed by several scampering emissaries.

The portal slammed shut with a thunderous boom. "No!" Bishop cried. "No! No! No!" The room was suddenly very silent.

Gary slowly stood up. Still dazed, he made his way to Bishop and lifted the bookcase off of his fallen friend. "What are we gonna do now?" he asked.

"We'll go after them as soon as Checkmate can open another portal."

Gary then walked over to Reprint, who was also somewhat wobbly after sustaining so severe a blow. "That can't happen for twenty four hours, Bish" Gary said. "What do we do until then?"

"We have a lot to do before then." Bishop was determined. "Because no matter what, I'm going to get Onyx and make him pay for everything he's done!"

# Chapter 13

## Expectations and Limitations

Shortly after his disastrous encounter with Onyx, Bishop called Miss Mann and asked her to come over as quickly as she could. She raced to the Chance house.

Bishop, Gary, Reprint and Miss Mann wasted no time exploring every inch of Onyx's hidden lair. But they didn't find anything they could use against their fearsome foe, or to change Justin back into a living boy again.

"When I woke up on my bed I didn't know where I was," Bishop said as the group returned to the living room. "Random must have changed me back and drugged me or something. At first I thought all of this had been a nightmare."

"It is a nightmare, Bish," Gary said.

Miss Mann sighed. "I can't believe Onyx has been right here, all along, pretending to be your grandfather. I'm so sorry. I failed Alabaster, and I failed you."

"You have my apologies, as well," Reprint said.

Miss Mann looked at the statue of Justin and shook her head. "Oh, Bishop. I shouldn't have let any of your friends get involved."

"You couldn't have stopped us," Gary insisted.

"Don't blame yourself, Miss Mann," Bishop said. "This isn't over yet."

Gary studied Aquarian's head, which now sat next to the motionless Checkmate on the chessboard. "Say, Miss Mann, I've been wondering. Where did Bishop's father make all these inventions and things of his?" he asked. "Did he have some sort of lab or something?"

"He never shared that information with me, or anyone else," Miss Mann replied.

Bishop shook his head. "There's nothing like that in the house. I would have found it by now."

Gary forged on. "You didn't know about Onyx's hidden lair under your house. So there could be a lab around here somewhere, right? Why don't you ask Checkmate? Or C.H.I.P.?"

"Onyx had access to C.H.I.P., and if C.H.I.P. had information about a laboratory Onyx would have found it," Bishop said. He turned to Checkmate and once again addressed the miniature king. "Checkmate, did my father have a hidden laboratory?"

Checkmate came instantly to life. "Yes. He did."

"Can you tell me where it is?" Bishop asked.

"Yes."

"Then tell me where it is!" Bishop screamed, his patience long gone.

"It is hidden behind the full-length mirror in the master bedroom. Go to it and you will find the letters of the alphabet engraved along its perimeter. Spell out your father's name by pressing the letters and you will find what you seek."

Bishop scowled. "There is nothing but an outside wall behind that mirror."

The miniature king shook his head. "That is incorrect. Alabaster utilized compressed space to create his workroom."

"Compressed space? What is that?" Bishop asked.

"It is difficult to explain in terms that you would understand. To put it simply, he borrowed space from one area and compressed it into another."

"Cool," Gary smiled. "Let's go see what he's talking about." He picked up Aquarian's head. "Maybe we'll find something in there that can help this poor guy."

Bishop and the others entered the sparsely furnished bedroom that had once been used by his parents but had been his grandfather's for most of his lifetime. They walked to a full-length mirror hanging in the far corner. Bishop took note of the engravings along its frame. It was with these very letters that he had first practiced the alphabet.

"I learned the alphabet studying these. My grandfather...I mean Onyx...taught...me..." Bishop stood silent as a flood of childhood memories washed over him. And then he cried, "My entire childhood was a lie! I hate Onyx! I hate him!"

Gary put his free hand on Bishop's shoulder. "Keep it together, Bish. Mandy needs you."

Bishop slowly touched the letters that spelled out his father's name. When the last letter was pressed the mirror slid sideways into the wall, revealing a hidden room. Just as Checkmate had explained, it was a fully equipped laboratory filled with devices from the Homeworld that Alabaster had re-created from memory. Some appeared to be futuristic, others surprisingly antiquated.

Bishop, Gary, Reprint and Miss Mann entered the room, which appeared to be larger than the entire house. It was windowless, lit only by glowing neon tubes and globes.

"This is incredible," Gary said.

Bishop was also in awe. "I can't believe this was here all this time."

"Alabaster was a lot smarter than everyone thought," Reprint mused.

Bishop took command. "Okay, everyone, look around for anything that might be useful to us."

Miss Mann suddenly gasped. Lying on a nearby table was an exact duplicate of Aquarian. The body was lifeless. Everyone gathered around the table, studying this new android.

Bishop touched the android's hand. "I wish there was some way we could bring you to life like your brother," he said.

A familiar voice suddenly rocked the room. "There is!"

"Checkmate? Is that you?" Bishop called out, looking everywhere at once.

The miniature king suddenly materialized on a nearby table. "I was created to assist Alabaster within this room," he announced.

Bishop leaned forward. "Do you know of a way to make this android come to life?"

Checkmate nodded. "The machine that you know as Aquarian was created within this room. You still have the head with the original programming inside it. We can download the information into the other unit."

"How?" Bishop asked.

Checkmate gestured to a set of shelves that were cluttered with all sorts of equipment. "Take the two caps on the shelf to your right and place one on each of their heads. Once this is done, just give the command and I will start the process of transference."

Gary placed Aquarian's head on the table next to the Aquarian double and attached the caps to the two android heads.

"Okay, Checkmate," Bishop said, adjusting the caps. "Begin the transference."

A low hum filled the room. The neon lights flickered. Gary and Reprint exchanged confused glances. They were both unsure about what they were watching.

A moment later, Checkmate spoke. "It is done!"

The new Aquarian opened his eyes as the hum subsided. "What happened?" he said, sitting up on the table. "The last thing I remember is being dropped from the sky."

"Your other body was destroyed," Bishop explained. "We've transferred you into this one. It seems my father made two of you. I wonder why he didn't activate you both?"

"The body you found here was the first one created and has certain limitations in it that the later model did not have," Checkmate said.

Aquarian looked down at his new body. "What type of limitations?" he asked with typical irritation.

"This unit lacks the strength that the later version possessed."

Aquarian jumped off the table and looked around. He was desperate to test himself. He grabbed Gary and tried to lift him off the ground.

"Hey!" Gary yelled. "What the heck are you doing?"

Try as he did, Aquarian could not move Gary. He suddenly looked very depressed. "It's true! I can't lift heavy objects anymore!"

"Hey! Watch who you're calling a heavy object," Gary snapped. "And let go of me!"

"This is terrible," Aquarian grumbled.

Miss Mann seemed unconcerned with Aquarian's distress. "It seems anything is possible within this room," she said as she looked about.

"Do you think so?" Bishop asked.

Miss Mann spread her arms wide as if embracing the room itself. "Look at how large this room is! Just think, Bishop. Your father created all this. He was truly a genius. I'm at a loss to explain his mastery of compressed space. Or his mastery of mind transference."

"Too bad he didn't master time, too," Gary said. "Then we could open another portal now, instead of waiting until tomorrow!"

Bishop stared at Gary. "Maybe we can! If the physical properties of space don't apply in here, maybe time isn't a factor, either. And besides, we're talking about moving between two worlds. Maybe they're in different time zones or something."

"You mean like Los Angeles?" Gary asked.

"Or like Australia," Bishop said. "It's already tomorrow night there, right? It could be next week in here! Or last year! Or never! Or always! Hey, Checkmate, what time is it in here?"

Checkmate shook his head. "That does not compute."

"See? I'm right!" Bishop declared. "Checkmate, can you open another portal in here?"

"Affirmative," Checkmate said. Unbeknownst to the others, Reprint dashed out of the room.

Miss Mann smiled. "Goodness, Bishop. You truly are your father's son."

Gary slapped Bishop on the back. "Guess some of my smarts are rubbing off on you, Bish."

Reprint returned to the room. He was dragging the statue of Justin. "If we're going to the Homeworld, we had better bring Justin with us," he said. "Maybe someone there can help him. Geez, he's heavy!"

Aquarian looked at Gary.

"Don't say it," Gary sneered.

"Okay, Checkmate, open a portal," Bishop commanded. "Right here, right now. I am also requesting that you open another portal in forty-eight Earth hours. In the living room, just to make sure we come back to the right place and time. I don't know if I even trust this room to be here."

As soon as Bishop stopped speaking a portal appeared. Miss Mann was momentarily awestruck.

"It has been so long since I have seen one of these," she whispered.

"Let's go!" Bishop commanded as he stepped into the portal. Gary and Reprint picked up the statue of Justin and followed. Aquarian was next. A wistful Miss Mann looked around the room then stepped through as well.

Seconds later, the portal closed with the usual thunderous boom.

# Chapter 14

## Brave New World

A small neon circle of light appeared in the middle of a sun-splashed meadow, growing ever wider until it resembled the inter-dimensional portals that had earlier opened in the Chance living room and in Alabaster's secret lab. Bishop and his friends stepped out of it, momentarily blinded by the brightness of the day. The meadow was surrounded on all sides by lush forests. A neon rainbow of a dozen different colors spanned the sky. The seemingly endless beauty around him stunned Bishop. Miss Mann was moved to quiet tears.

"Is...is this the Homeworld?" Bishop asked.

"It's exactly as I remember," Miss Mann said, her voice barely rising above a whisper. "Exactly as we left it."

Bishop was awestruck. "It's...amazing."

"Is that Bishop's castle?" Gary said, pointing to a glistening white structure on a distant mountain.

"Yes, it is," Miss Mann replied. "Alabaster must have programmed Checkmate to deliver us right here."

"Dad thought of everything didn't he?" Bishop said, almost sadly.

A familiar voice growled from behind them. "Not everything, you little rodent!"

Bishop whirled around and found himself face to face with Random.

"Random!" Bishop yelled. His eyes fell on her bandaged shoulder.

"In the flesh, sugar," Random replied. "And none the worse for wear." She looked behind Bishop and eyed the statue of Justin. "It looks like one of you brought a statue for our fountain. How nice. We'll keep it to remember you after you're all dead. Which should be any minute now."

"Not if I can help it!" Reprint cried. He scrambled up a rock and leapt into the air. But instead of changing into Peter Pan, as he had planned, he swiftly fell to the ground.

"Something wrong?" Random laughed.

"I can't change form," Reprint sputtered.

Print appeared from behind Random. "I think my brother is discovering what we already know. None of us have any of our Earth powers here. We lost them when we crossed over."

Miss Mann frantically waved her hands. Nothing happened. "It's true!" she said. "I can't create anything!"

"Does this mean you can't change Justin back?" Bishop asked Random.

"Afraid not. Not that I would have, mind you."

"Where's Onyx?" Bishop demanded. "And Mandy?"

"Onyx knew you would follow him here, sugar. He's waiting. And so is your little girlfriend." Random waved a strange looking gun at Bishop and the others. "Follow us or die. Now!"

"I wish I had my strength," Aquarian said. "I'd stop you cold."

Random smiled. "Hmm. You rebuilt the little pest. How convenient. He can help carry the statue. Now get moving or die. This is your final chance, Chance." Bishop frowned. Random chuckled at her little joke. Then she turned to Miss Mann.

"I haven't seen you in ages, Christie Rae," she snarled. "You look exhausted."

Miss Mann studied her adversary. "Random, you are still the same vile shrew."

The group marched for several miles at gunpoint through the forest, finally arriving at a dark castle. It was very different from the castle they had seen earlier. While the other glistened in the sun, this one seemed to absorb light. It was covered with mold and dead vines on the exterior and it was surrounded by a stagnant moat. The entrance resembled a dark, foreboding cave. The walls and floor were covered with grime. There were enormous cobwebs everywhere. Gary briefly freaked when he realized that a giant spider, at least two feet wide, was sitting in one of the webs, watching him.

Random and Print lead their prisoners up several flights of stairs and into a dank, foul smelling room. Two large windows provided the only light. The door slammed behind them. Aquarian and Reprint set the statue that had been Justin on the floor.

Onyx stepped through another door at the far end of the room. "Onyx, don't you ever get tired of your pathetic little games?" Miss Mann asked, a dollop of condescension in her voice. She then glanced at Random. "Or your pathetic women?"

"Dear, dear Christie Rae," Onyx replied. "It was so amusing, watching you scamper about Wellington, lost without your leader. You were always so polite to doddering old Andrew Chance when you saw him. If only you'd known that it was I all that time, watching you and having a grand laugh. Thank you for keeping me entertained all those years on that tiresome world."

"You are as low as ever," Miss Mann replied, her tone now one of anger.

"You'll find that I haven't lost my flair. I still have entertaining ways of extinguishing people's mundane lives, which you shall find out very shortly." Onyx was face to face with Miss Mann. "As you have figured out by now, we have all lost our powers here. I look forward to returning to Earth one day and claiming it as my own, with the help of updated technology from this world, my loyal emissaries and, of course, the support of my loving nephew."

"I will never side with you!" Bishop exclaimed. "Never!"

"I think you'll come around," Onyx said as he waved his hand. An obedient emissary Bishop recognized as Silhouette sprang forward and threw a switch on a control panel. A wall slid away, revealing another room beyond. There, in the center of the room, was Mandy, trapped within a cage and suspended from the ceiling. Beneath the cage were swirling rings of neon energy.

"Mandy!" Bishop called out. "Are you okay?"

"Yes! Don't worry about me! You've got to stop Onyx!"

"Don't even think about trying to approach her, nephew," Onyx warned. He then grabbed Silhouette and shoved him into the neon rings. There was an explosion of neon sparks upon contact, accompanied by a deafening crackling noise. Silhouette screamed in agony as the neon coursed through him, reducing him to ashes.

Bishop and his friends were horrified. "You are still the most unholy of monsters," an outraged Miss Mann hissed.

"Just one of the perks of the job," Onyx chuckled. He stood directly in front of Bishop, seemingly towering over the boy. "Now then, nephew, behave yourself, or I will light up your girlfriend, as well." Bishop remained silent. Onyx then walked slowly around the room, finally stopping next to a large laser gun perched upon a pedestal. It was aimed outside an open window. Next to the pedestal was a large computer console.

"This room contains one of the greatest arsenals ever created on this world!" Onyx said. "How I missed it during my long stay on Earth. The emissaries I left behind have kept everything in working order. My weapons are all controlled by this computer, which is keyed to my voice only. So you see, Bishop, scientific genius runs in the family. Watch closely as I finally take what is rightfully mine."

"Stalemate," Onyx said to his computer, "prepare firing sequence Onyx One." He pointed to a monitor on one wall. Alabaster's glistening white castle appeared on the screen. "We'll begin by destroying this eyesore."

"If you've always had access to this much fire power, why have you waited until now to use it?" Bishop asked. "Why didn't you use it earlier?"

"When it came to technology, your father and I were too evenly matched. With Alabaster in charge, I could never get the upper hand. And then we all were trapped on your miserable world. Now, my brother is gone, and I am back, and I have the element of surprise! Your father's precious kingdom won't know what hit it. Do you have any last words, nephew?"

"Yes," Bishop yelled out. "I wish that your computer would crash itself!"

Onyx's computer suddenly began crackling, sending a shower of sparks into the air. Onyx was enraged.

"Blast you, boy!" Onyx screamed. "You were supposed to be powerless here! Just like the rest of us!"

"Good heavens!" Miss Mann exclaimed. "Since your parents were from both worlds, you must be able to carry over your power from one to the other!"

Onyx quickly punched a few buttons on the keyboard. "I don't think the damage is too severe. It looks like I'll get the last laugh after all." He pressed a button and the laser fired.

A building near Alabaster's castle exploded into pieces. Bishop and the others watched the destruction on the monitor.

"Accursed machine!" Onyx screamed. "I was aiming for the castle!" He tried typing in a few more commands, but there was no response from the computer.

"Why don't you just give up?" Gary said. "You'll never succeed while we're around to stop you."

Random aimed her laser gun at Gary. "That can be rectified, big boy!" she snarled.

Aquarian pushed Gary out of the way as Random fired. The laser beam grazed Gary's arm. He yelped and fell to the floor. Random turned her gun toward Aquarian and fired once again. She missed, but the beam struck the neon coils under the cage in which Mandy was imprisoned. There was another explosion of neon sparks and arcs. Mandy screamed. The coils were in some sort of meltdown, sending deadly neon arcs in every direction.

Amid the chaos, Reprint surprised his brother and slammed his fist into Print's jaw, knocking him out. Aquarian, meanwhile, grabbed Random's gun. The two struggled, and Random appeared to have the upper hand, until she was struck in the back by a neon arc. She released the gun and screamed as the neon seared her flesh. Smoldering, she dashed to Onyx's side.

Aquarian handed Bishop the gun. He aimed it at Onyx.

"Stalemate, cut the power to those coils. Now!" Bishop commanded.

On command, Stalemate emitted a low hum, and the neon coils under Mandy's cage simply disappeared.

"Lower the cage. Slowly!" Bishop continued.

"Insolent whelp! I won't allow this," Onyx roared as the cage slowly dropped toward the floor.

Onyx stepped forward, prompting Bishop to fire the laser. The beam passed between Random and Onyx, narrowly missing both of them. Onyx froze.

"Reprint," Bishop commanded. "Get Mandy out of that thing."

Bishop kept the gun on Onyx and Random as Reprint ran to the cage, which was now just a few inches above the floor. He opened it, and Mandy jumped out.

"Are you hurt, Mandy?" Miss Mann asked.

"No, but Gary is," Mandy said. She ran to her fallen friend, who was lying on the floor holding his injured arm. He was losing blood. "Oh, Gary, I'm so sorry." With great care, Mandy slowly lifted Gary's arm. It suddenly stopped bleeding.

"What's happening?" a dazed Gary moaned.

Mandy didn't respond. She continued to concentrate on Gary. The burnt area on his arm began to turn a healthy pink. Within seconds there was no sign of any injury.

Gary was now quite agitated. "What did you do?"

Without saying a word, Mandy stepped away from Gary. She was standing next to the statue of Justin.

"I think I know," Miss Mann said. "The same forces that enabled us to acquire specific powers on your world must also work for you Earthlings on this one. Upon entering this world, all of you acquired powers of your own. Mandy must have the power of healing."

"How revolting," Random sniffed.

"Quickly, Mandy," Miss Mann said. "See if you can heal Justin."

Mandy placed her hand on the statue of Justin and, sure enough, he returned to life.

"This is going from bad to worse," Random sighed.

"Where am I?" Justin asked as he stumbled about, shaking off the after effects of his ordeal.

"Long story there, dude," Gary said.

"We're on Alabaster's Homeworld," Mandy explained. "Random turned you into a statue."

Justin's voice was shaky. "The last thing I remember is being in Bishop's house. I went there to tell you all something. I...I was helping Onyx all along."

"What?" Gary yelped.

Random shook her head. "You can't get good help these days."

"Shut up," Bishop snapped. "Justin, what are you talking about?"

"He was following all of you, through me. He said that he would kill me if I didn't help him. I never should have let him get away with it. I...didn't realize...how much you all meant to me." Justin turned to Onyx. "As for you, you old loser, I wish I had hit you over the head even harder!"

"So you are the coward who struck me from behind!" Onyx scowled. "You will die for that, you miserable little traitor."

"I hope you can all forgive me," Justin said to his friends.

Mandy was sympathetic. "There is nothing to forgive. It wasn't your fault. Onyx threatened you!"

"Mandy's right," Bishop added. "You had no choice."

Justin suddenly turned pale.

"Are you alright?" Mandy asked.

"I don't feel so good," Justin groaned, placing a hand on his chest. "My whole body is tingling."

Small black and gray hairs began sprouting all over Justin's arms, chest and face. His ears and nose started growing and his legs seemed to shorten. Justin let out a scream—actually, more of a howl—and fell to the floor. His hands and feet changed into paws. He grew a small tail.

Justin had become a wolf.

"What have you done to him, you psycho?" Gary screamed at Onyx.

"This is not my doing, enlarged one."

Wolf-Justin walked to Bishop's side, sniffed at Onyx and growled.

Bishop was still holding Random's gun. He spoke clearly and directly with newfound confidence. "It would appear, Uncle Evil, that you are finally beaten. If any of you makes a move, I'll shoot you. Or Justin will rip your throats out. Reprint, find something to tie these creeps up with."

Gary leaned toward Bishop, speaking quietly into his ear. "Uh, Bish, that won't work. Rope? Shape shifter? Been there, done that? Got our butts whipped?"

"I think rope will hold them on this world," Bishop asserted. "Onyx can't shape shift here." Reprint left in search of rope.

Mandy knelt next to Wolf-Justin. "Justin? Can you understand me?" she asked.

Wolf-Justin placed his head in Mandy's hands.

Mandy started to pet him. "You poor thing," she sighed.

Gary laughed. "If he doesn't change back, can I keep him as a pet?" Justin growled in protest.

Amid all the excitement nobody had kept watch over Print, who had regained consciousness. As the others were talking, Print snuck up behind them and lunged at Bishop. Aquarian thwarted Print's assault, but the distraction was long enough for Onyx to shove Random aside and grab Mandy, wrapping one arm around her neck.

"I believe we have an old-fashioned stand off, nephew," Onyx smiled. "One wrong move and I'll snap her tender little neck."

Bishop didn't reply. He simply glared at Onyx with pure hatred in his eyes.

"Now then," Onyx continued, "I want you to use your power and command Stalemate to destroy your father's castle."

"Never!" Bishop shouted.

"Then say good-bye to your girlfriend," Onyx said, in a tone so chilling it kept everyone frozen where they stood. Wolf-Justin growled.

Onyx's arm tightened around Mandy's neck. "I mean it, nephew. I will kill her."

Bishop caved. "No, don't! I'll do it! I'll do it!"

"Bishop, you can't!" Mandy cried. "What about all the people?"

With his head bowed down in defeat, Bishop silently walked to Stalemate.

"You can't trust him, Bish!" Gary called out. "How do you know he'll let her go?" Bishop ignored his friend.

Reprint returned carrying a length of rope. He stopped cold when he saw Onyx back in charge, with Print at his side. "Oh, no," he whispered.

"Drop the rope, bro," Print ordered. "You won't be needing it."

Bishop stood in front of Stalemate. He looked at Mandy. Their eyes met for a long moment. Bishop smiled weakly at her, and then looked down at the computer.

"Okay, I guess I have no other choice," Bishop said. "Stalemate, destroy the castle."

"Specify castle," Stalemate replied.

Bishop paused for a moment, and then a small smile came upon his face. "This one! Destroy it! Now!" he demanded.

Stalemate unleashed the full force of the laser on Onyx's castle. The giant gun began rotating, firing in all directions. A shocked Onyx released Mandy and grabbed Bishop.

"You fool!" Onyx roared. "Reverse your command! Now!"

"Too late, uncle! Get out, everybody! Now!"

Sections of the ceiling began falling to the floor as the laser kept turning and firing. It was destroying the castle. Several of Onyx's emissaries were crushed under falling debris. Miss Mann grabbed Gary and Mandy and led them to a doorway. Onyx shoved Bishop aside and feverishly worked at the computer.

"Print!" Onyx commanded. "Get over here and help me!"

A laser blast exploded just above Print, showering him with rubble.

"Bag that! I'm outta here!" Print said as he dashed out of the room.

Reprint ran after Print. "You can't escape, brother!"

"Bishop!" Mandy cried. She was unable to see him through the falling debris.

"He'll be okay," Miss Mann insisted. "Come with me!"

"No way!" Gary said. "I'm staying with Bish!"

"No, Gary," Bishop yelled. "This is my fight! Go!"

Mandy reached for Wolf-Justin. "Come on, boy."

Neither Wolf-Justin nor Mandy noticed a large section of the ceiling falling in their direction. Only Aquarian saw it. He pushed Wolf-Justin, Mandy, Gary and Miss Mann through the doorway as it crashed to the floor, burying Aquarian and blocking the exit.

Mandy was horrified. "We've got to help Aquarian!"

"No!" Miss Mann said. "We've got to get out of here! Now!"

Onyx, meanwhile, abandoned Stalemate. He was seething. He was now trapped in the crumbling room with Bishop and Random. A beam fell onto Random, striking her arm and causing her to drop her gun. Random wasn't hurt, but the beam smashed her gun. She turned to Onyx. "What are we going to do now?"

Onyx looked to the window. "We can jump into the moat."

"Great idea, sugar. But I can't swim."

"I can," Bishop said as he tried to cross to the window. But Random was too fast. She grabbed him and held his neck so tightly that her nails pierced his skin.

"You're not going anywhere, honey," she purred. "You're gonna die here."

"Release the boy!" Onyx commanded. "Now!"

"No!" Random was defiant. "With him dead, we can start over again! There will be no one to stop us!"

"This is not open to debate," Onyx said as he ripped Random away from Bishop. The boy stumbled to the open window as bricks and beams rained down around him. Random looked into Onyx's eyes.

"You promised me that we would be together forever, sugar. I intend to hold you to your word."

Random grabbed onto Onyx and kissed him with great passion. He shoved her away, sending her into the shadow of a crumbling wall. Random screamed as the wall fell, crushing her. Bishop could only stare at Onyx. "This is not over!" Onyx roared as another explosion sent the remaining ceiling crashing down on him. Within seconds, all that Bishop could see of his uncle was one still hand sticking out from under a pile of rubble.

Bishop seemingly had two choices. Die in the fire that was sweeping through the room, or be buried alive as the castle continued to crumble. Bishop chose a third option and jumped out the window, certain he would land in the moat below. An entire wing of the castle exploded behind him as he fell through the air. Bishop shielded himself as debris flew past him on all sides. He finally splashed into the moat, but he was not out of danger. Further sections of the castle rained down around him. Bishop disappeared beneath the surface.

Miss Mann, Mandy, Gary and Reprint watched in horror from a safe distance. Wolf-Justin cowered behind them. As the dust and debris began to settle, Miss Mann and the others dashed toward the moat, desperately looking around for Bishop. Mandy was crying. Gary was teary eyed too.

Miss Mann halted. Ahead of them, at the water's edge, a dazed Bishop splashed to the surface, gasping for air. "Bishop!" Mandy cried. Just as Bishop began crawling out of the moat, massive explosions rocked the remaining towers that comprised Onyx's vast castle. Bishop and the others could only stare as the entire structure blew apart and crumbled into the murky water.

"How did you survive under all that, Bish?" Gary asked. "It looked like you were buried alive!"

As if on cue, Aquarian surfaced next to Bishop.

Bishop smiled. "You can thank Aquarian. As soon as I hit the water he was there. He shielded me with his body and found an area under there where we wouldn't be crushed. Good thing I'm on the swim team. I was able to keep up with him and hold my breath until we were safe. Aquarian, I owe you my life. You saved me."

"Your father saved you," Aquarian replied. "Remember, he created me to help you."

"Did either of you see Onyx down there?" Miss Mann asked.

"Onyx and Random are dead," Bishop said. "I saw them die. My last living relative is gone." Bishop looked down, lost in the sadness of his sudden realization. "Now I really am alone."

"You will never be alone, Bishop," Miss Mann said. "Your father and mother will always be with you. And so will your loyal subjects. You've just taken the first steps to becoming a great leader.

"Come, let me show you to your castle, my king."

# Chapter 15

## All Together Now

Bishop, Miss Mann, Mandy, Gary, Aquarian, Wolf-Justin and Reprint, with a bound and gagged Print in tow, stood at the front gates of Bishop's kingdom. The gates were oversized and made of solid gold. Inside, white brick streets were lined with multi-colored flowerbeds. Tall, shiny buildings rose to meet the blue, cloudless sky. Twin neon rainbows stretched overhead from horizon to horizon.

"Welcome to the Kingdom of New Hopes," Miss Mann said. "Nobody wants for anything here. Everyone has enough to eat and a place to live. Everybody helps out their neighbors if they are in need. Ah, it is so wonderful to walk these streets again."

"What if somebody doesn't feel like helping out or working?" Gary asked.

"We do not have that problem here. Everybody contributes something to the society because they feel that their society is a reflection of themselves. The more they put into it, the more they can enjoy it."

Bishop regarded the splendor before him. "I thought my father said that this world was war torn," he said.

"It was, before we all left for your world. But Alabaster made certain that the kingdom itself was well protected from the evil forces that surrounded it. Apparently, with Onyx out of the way all those years, peace returned to our land. That was your father's legacy."

"I can't believe Onyx's emissaries just waited around for him to return," Bishop said. "He was gone for 14 years!"

Miss Mann stopped walking and turned to Bishop. "Onyx was evil personified," she exclaimed. "Men with power as unholy as his can easily influence those less willful. His followers felt that they had no choice but to remain loyal, even during his prolonged absence."

"What country are we in?" Mandy asked.

"This world has no countries," Miss Mann replied. "Only this one kingdom. You wouldn't know it to look around here, but the rest of this planet is uninhabitable. We are surrounded on all sides by great oceans.

"The oceans on this planet are very dangerous," Miss Mann continued. "Only a few brave souls have dared explore them, and most of them were never heard from again." Miss Mann fluttered her arms, as if to clear away cobwebs, or bad memories. "Those stories are best left for another day. Right now, we must celebrate being here in this wonderful place!"

Dozens of people turned out to greet them as they walked through the streets. Everyone seemed to be in perfect health and in good spirits. Many people recognized Miss Mann. Eventually Bishop and his friends arrived at Alabaster's castle. It was the largest building in the kingdom. Two older men greeted them.

"May we help you?" one of the men asked

The second man was studying Miss Mann closely. "Christie Rae? Is that you?"

Miss Mann recognized him immediately. "Oh my stars! Castleton!" she exclaimed, embracing him as one would an old friend.

"It's been so long! We had given you all up for lost!" Castleton said.

"It's a long story," Miss Mann replied. "I'll tell you all about it later."

"Christie Rae, you're just as beautiful as ever!"

"And you're still the flirt!"

"Where is King Alabaster?" Castleton asked.

Miss Mann lowered her head. So, too, did Bishop. Castleton understood.

"This is his son. Bishop, this is Castleton, your father's most trusted aide."

Castleton bowed. "Ah, young king, how good to meet you. I am sorry to hear of your loss. Our loss, I should say. I see quite a bit of your father in you."

Bishop could only smile. He was flattered, but he was also exhausted. "It's nice to meet you, Castleton," he said. "These are my friends, Gary, Mandy and Reprint. And this is Aquarian."

Castleton eyed Aquarian closely. "An android, I wager."

"How can you tell?" Bishop asked.

"I believe I helped your father with his original concept for this one," Castleton answered, still regarding Aquarian with quiet awe. "Perhaps I can remove a limb or two and see how Alabaster improved on our original design."

"Try it and I shall remove your limbs as well," Aquarian said with perfect clarity.

Castleton beamed. "Ah ha! Alabaster programmed you for self-preservation. Leave it to your father to enhance an already magnificent creation." Castleton turned back to Bishop and Miss Mann. "You all must be tired. I will have rooms made ready for you, and fresh clothing."

Reprint stepped forward, pulling Print behind him. "We'll need to find a cell for my brother here. He's one of Onyx's men."

Castleton took Miss Mann aside. "Yes, what of Onyx? When those lasers were fired from the direction of his lair, we feared the worst. We lost a warehouse. Luckily nobody was inside."

"Onyx was on Earth with us for all those years," Miss Mann replied. "He recently returned, but he's dead now. Bishop saved our world."

Bishop and his friends were treated like royalty from that moment on. Castleton led Bishop on a tour of the castle, including Alabaster's study. Bishop admired a portrait of his father hanging on the wall amid those of previous rulers. He was later presented with Alabaster's retractable white sword, still in working order. Mandy was offered her choice of fine dresses. Gary took an extensive tour of the kitchens and enjoyed a lavish feast. Technicians tuned up and polished Aquarian. Reprint explored the royal library and found dozens of books about the history of the Homeworld. He was determined to read them all. Wolf-Justin was given a bath and a flea dip.

The following morning Bishop awoke totally refreshed. He had slept later than he usually did at home. He was wearing a pair of blue silk pajamas befitting a king.

As he surveyed the spacious bedroom he saw beautifully carved wooden furniture that looked to be hundreds of years old. On the opposite wall was a painting of his father sitting on an animal that resembled a six-legged horse. He hadn't noticed these furnishings when he retired the night before, due to sheer exhaustion. He wondered if this room had been his father's bedroom.

The bedroom door opened. A dark haired boy wearing a shiny lime green outfit entered. He was carrying a large basket.

"Good morning, your majesty," the boy said. "I've brought you new clothing."

Bishop climbed out of bed. "Thanks, uh…"

"Diggory, your majesty. My family has worked for your family for over twenty generations."

Bishop took the basket of clothing from Diggory and placed it on the bed. He looked inside. "Thanks, Diggory, but I'd rather have the clothes I came here with."

Diggory looked puzzled. "Aren't you pleased with the clothing I picked out? If you don't like the colors, I'm sure I can find others that you will like. Give me time. I'll serve you well."

Bishop shook his head. "No, the colors are fine. But everything has been changing so quickly lately that I would feel more comfortable wearing my own clothes for now."

Diggory nodded. "If that is what you wish, I will get your uniform for you. It has been laundered."

As Diggory turned to leave, Bishop called to him. "Wait. There is something you can do for me."

Diggory smiled, eager to please. "Yes, sire?"

"Call me Bishop."

"Of course, sire," Diggory said. "I mean, Bishop. What else do you need?"

"I just need someone to answer some questions."

"Questions?"

"I've never been a king before, and I don't know what's involved. I don't know if I'm up to it. I mean, everyone thinks I came here looking to get my birthright."

"Didn't you?"

"No. Not really. I just came here to find out about my father. He died when I was very young. I knew nothing about him when I started this quest, but I've learned so much. He wasn't too different from me. He tried his best. Sometimes he succeeded and other times he didn't. But the most important thing is that he never gave up or stopped trying. He had his hopes and beliefs and never stopped working towards them. I think if there is one thing he wanted me to understand while I was on this quest, then that would be it. Now it's time to return home."

"But what about all your royal duties?" Diggory asked. "You have a lot of catching up to do."

"That's my point. I never asked for any of this. If I stayed here, I'd feel like I was running away from my problems back home. It's time that I started to face up to them and overcome them. I'm not very good with my schoolwork. I'm on the swim team, but I always seem to mess that up, too. But now I think I understand why. I didn't know who I was or what I was."

Bishop paused. Diggory wondered if he should say anything. Then Bishop continued. "The first thing I've got to do when I go back is find out if Onyx left any emissaries on Earth." Bishop thought for a second and smiled. "Also, there's somebody back home that I would miss if I stayed here."

"Would that be Miss Conway?"

Bishop laughed. "Is it that obvious?"

"Not to everyone. But I've been trained to be observant. I can understand why you wish to return home, but I am sorry to see you leave. I was hoping to carry on the family tradition."

"Don't worry. I didn't say that I'm never coming back. I can come back whenever I want to visit, now that I control the portal."

That afternoon, Bishop and his friends relaxed in the castle gardens. Bishop and Miss Mann sat on plush chairs, while across the yard; Mandy and Gary were playing with Wolf-Justin. Reprint was laying on the grass with a stack of books next him.

Bishop turned to Miss Mann. "This place is great, but I think we should go back home," he said. "As much as I would like to stay, I have to go back and seek out any emissaries that stayed behind. It's my responsibility to deal with them."

"It sounds as if you've given the matter a great deal of thought," Miss Mann observed.

"Also, until I discover how to open a portal from this world, the only way I have of traveling between the two worlds is back home," Bishop continued. "I have a portal scheduled to open soon. Mandy's and Gary's folks must be worried sick. Justin is probably anxious to ditch the wolf thing."

Miss Mann watched Wolf-Justin romp on the lawn. "Oh, I don't know. He seems rather happy to me." She had barely finished talking when Wolf-Justin began acting strangely. His wolf hair started to disappear. He howled as his nose and ears shrank and his arms and legs returned to human form. Within moments, Justin was standing on two feet again.

"Apparently I spoke too soon," Miss Mann said.

"Justin! You're back!" Mandy exclaimed.

"Yeah, and you're naked!" Gary laughed.

Justin blushed a furious shade of red. Mandy and Miss Mann turned away. Gary laughed so hard that he fell to the ground. Reprint looked up briefly and then turned his attention back to his books. Bishop removed a tablecloth from a nearby table and brought it to Justin.

"It looks like you're gonna have to work on controlling that power of yours," Bishop said.

An embarrassed Justin quickly wrapped the cloth around himself.

Moments later, Castleton arrived with a freshly tuned up Aquarian. "I have been working on your friend," Castleton said. "I've made a few upgrades to his program, but I was unable to increase his strength. Perhaps if I had more time I could more fully enhance him."

Miss Mann broke the news of their impending departure to her old friend. "I'm afraid Bishop and his friends have to return to Earth."

"But you just got here, my king. Do you have to leave so soon?"

"I'm afraid so, Castleton."

"Reprint and I will stay behind and help out in your absence," Miss Mann said.

"Aren't you going to continue teaching, Miss Mann?" Mandy asked. "I mean, now that Bishop is king and Onyx is gone, won't you be returning to Earth?"

"Eventually," Miss Mann replied. "But I have been gone too long and there are things that need my attention here." Miss Mann was silent for a moment. "I am very proud of all of you," she said. "I am honored to know such fine people."

"If it is all the same to you, I'd like to stay behind, too," Justin said.

Bishop was shocked. "Don't you want to go home?"

"There isn't much of a home for me to go back to. My parents lead separate lives. They've been arguing about who gets stuck with me. I don't think either one will miss me. And besides, maybe I can master this wolf thing. I'll bet I could learn to control changing back and forth. It could be cool. I'll go back again. Someday. Maybe on your next trip."

"Justin, are you sure about this?" Mandy asked.

"Yeah. You all go on without me. You can always come back and visit. Bishop knows the way." Justin shook Bishop's hand. "You had better get going before you miss your portal."

"You're a good friend, Justin," Bishop said. "A great friend, I mean. The best."

Bishop faced the entire group. "In fact, you are all great friends. I'm a very lucky king! Now, let's go. We have a portal to get to. Aquarian, do you want to stay here, too?"

"No," Aquarian replied, shaking his head. "You n ay not be out of danger yet. If any of Onyx's emissaries remain on Earth, you will need me to protect you."

"This isn't fair," Gary moaned.

"What's the matter?" Bishop asked.

"All you guys got neat powers when we came here, and I got none."

Miss Mann put her hand on Gary's shoulder. "Don't worry Gary. These powers manifest themselves at different times in different people. It can take awhile before your power comes into being."

"It's still not fair," Gary grumbled.

Castleton stepped forward. "I have a vehicle waiting to take you back to the meadow, my king."

"Thank you, Castleton. Okay, guys. Let's do it."

Mandy hugged Justin. A reluctant Gary hugged him, as well. The vehicle floated toward them. Bishop noted that it resembled an automobile without wheels. A series of different colored lights that pulsated at a fast speed circled its undercarriage. Once the vehicle landed, Bishop, Mandy, Gary and Aquarian stepped aboard. Then it silently ascended and pulled away. The four friends waved to Justin, Castleton, Miss Mann and Reprint. Castleton saluted. Bishop returned the gesture as he marveled once again at the beauty of his new home. Or was it a home away from home? This was one of many questions Bishop knew he would have to address in the weeks ahead.

Once again, a portal opened in Bishop's living room. Bishop, Mandy, Gary and Aquarian stepped through. The portal remained open.

"We're back, guys," Bishop said. "Mission accomplished!"

"Cool. I could get used to this," Gary declared.

Bishop smiled. "If all goes well, maybe you will."

"I've got to get home," Mandy sighed.

"Me, too," Gary said. "Mom and Dad must be freaking! Bish, man, we're gonna have to talk about all this, and I mean everything, real soon!"

"We will, buddy."

"You know, I don't really have any reason to stay here," Bishop said. "In fact, this house gives me the creeps. Could I stay at your place for a while, Gary? Your family has always been like a second family to me."

"Sure, Bish. We'll tell my parents that your grandfather had to go out of town. Way out of town! Stay as long as you want."

"What about me?" Aquarian inquired.

"You can come along too," Gary said. "We'll say you're Bishop's weird cousin or something."

And with that, Bishop, Gary, Mandy and Aquarian walked out the front door and into the light of a sunny day. Bishop was happy to be back on Earth, even if his life had changed forever. He looked at Mandy and reached for her hand as they strolled down the front walk. Mandy responded by wrapping her arms around Bishop and kissing him.

Gary turned away. "Hey, guys, c'mon. You're embarrassing me."

Bishop was speechless. He gazed into Mandy's eyes and smiled. For the first time ever, his life seemed to be filled with exciting new possibilities.

Meanwhile, back in the Chance living room, a dark figure appeared in the portal. A hand reached out and grabbed the white king from the chessboard.

"Checkmate!" a voice declared.

Sinister laughter filled the room as the portal closed with a thunderous boom.

**THE END**

**(for now)**

If you enjoyed the adventures of Bishop and his friends, then look for upcoming stories in the series. For more information please visit our website at **www.thelastchance.com**.

### "Second Chance"
The Last Chance II

Bishop and his friends encounter a mysterious young boy from the Homeworld who claims to be Bishop's brother. And they also meet, the enigmatic BJ, a traveler from the future.

### "Chance Encounter"
The Last Chance III

Bishop and his companions must save the Homeworld when the line between fantasy and reality begin to blur.

### "Lost Chances"
The Last Chance IV

Bishop travels back in time with his friends to try and prevent the death of his parents.

**"Take the Chance"**
The Last Chance V

Bishop's secret is exposed when he is kidnapped by a covert government organization that plans to use him for its own sinister agenda.

# About the Authors

### James Gauthier
James Gauthier has served as a consultant to writers of comic books and syndicated comic strips. The Last Chance is his first novel.

### Ed Martin
Ed Martin is a journalist and television critic who has written for USA Today, TV Guide and Advertising Age, among other publications. He is also the author of several screenplays. The Last Chance is his first novel.

# About the Artists

### Frank Bolle
Veteran artist Frank Bolle is one of the most prolific comic book artists of all time. He worked for Western Publishing, illustrating science fiction strips like Buck Rogers, Flash Gordon and Dr. Solar in addition to Boys Life, the Boy Scout magazine. Bolle drew The Heart of Juliet Jones for King Features from 1984 to 1999, and the long-running soap-opera strip Winnie Winkle. He currently draws Apartment 3-G a syndicated newspaper strip.

Bolle lives in Connecticut with his wife, Lori. He is president of Connecticut Classic Arts and is a member of the National Cartoonists

by Jack Kirby and Steve Ditko. For three years, he attended the School of Visual Arts in New York, where he was taught by Will Eisner and Harvey Kurtzman. He then apprenticed at Neal Adams' and Dick Giordano's Continuity Associates. In no time, he was inking DC's Legion of Super Heroes. His first Marvel Comics assignment, "Guardians of the Galaxy" in Marvel Presents, launched a career that has made him one of comics' most sought after inkers. His long list of credits includes Star Wars, Spider-Woman, Man-Thing, Power Pack and X-Men. Artistically he's been influenced by "everybody" from the aforementioned Ditko and Kirby to Jim Steranko, Berni Wrightson, Howard Chaykin, Walt Simonson, Craig Russell and Steve Leialoha. He lives in upstate New York with his wife, Ann, and his son, Ian.

0-595-27913-9